ONE OR ANOTHER

For Michael,
affectionately
and
with due respect—

Rosalyn

Also by Rosalyn Drexler

I AM THE BEAUTIFUL STRANGER

THE LINE OF LEAST EXISTENCE
AND OTHER PLAYS

ONE OR ANOTHER

rosalyn drexler

E. P. DUTTON & CO., INC., NEW YORK, 1970

[01]

For Danny

One or another
Is lost, since we fall apart
Endlessly, in one motion depart
From each other.

                      —D. H. Lawrence

ONE OR ANOTHER

J folded a small piece of orange origami paper into a lobster. He can do intricate things with his hands. It surprised me.

Origami: orgasm, orange, outrage, gamy, aura: J created.

The lobster lies on a pile of books on my desk: the topmost one is *The Valadon Drama*. If the lobster did not have two long pointed feelers; it would look like an armadillo; it is accordion pleated from the tip of its tail to its middle.

Dear J,

I didn't expect it. And I didn't want it. And it came and dumped itself on my couch. Without shoes. With socks. Buried in a book. Was it shy? Or what was it? A worm? I thought, ". . . almost a worm. . . ." No beginning, no end, all sex. I saw,

13

as it uncoiled its flesh, that it was all sex: that it crawled into me and disappeared. Where's that worm now? I'm going nuts with the advent of the worm. I love you.

◉

J's mother: June Wolff. The entire bookcase in her foyer is full of shells: the crusty abodes of sea creatures in company with fish skeletons, brittle beetles, fossils, sand dollars and pieces of metal or wood that June thinks resemble art. All lie together displayed with exquisite taste on mahogany shelves. All dead. The opposite of June Wolff. Perhaps not. There is nothing so exclusive, alone, or tight as a dancer . . . always perfecting their bodies; never satisfied; punishing themselves, attempting to defy natural laws, e.g., to outwit gravity and death by constantly moving! The movement is a screen behind which the dancer lies dying; and the shells on June's shelves are the screens of her life fanning out a small translucent span of beauty.

J resembles June: same eyes, same thick mouth. But the child, that is, J, does not dance.

In the coldest weather, J would not wear undershirts. And he'd forget to put his sweater on. Or, he'd leave his jacket unzipped. I was almost afraid to offer him a sweater. He accepted the imported double-knit black turtleneck woolen sweater when I showed it to him. And kept it for a few weeks. When I got it back, the smell of sweat was evident. I put it on and lowered my head toward my armpit so that I could smell him.

My husband, M, has a full red beard and a long red moustache. He is in the habit of pulling the hairs of his beard out one by one as he writes. The tiny, prickly pain keeps him alert.

To the Editor:
It seems to me that the "militant student" of today is nothing more than the "juvenile delinquent" of a decade ago. He should be dealt with swiftly and firmly in whatever way necessary to halt the destruction of private property, the interference with the right of other students to go to classes, and the willful disruption of the ROTC program, which so many of our clean-cut, diligent youth take part in

15

to serve their country. The police who stand between us and the dissidents have shown remarkable self-control by using clubs at the ready, instead of pistols. I suggest that if the SDS continues its bullying tactics on campus, that we the citizens join in with government forces, and bring the Students for the Destruction of a Democratic Society to their knees with a pistol at their temples. This is the only way to treat those who would destroy all our forefathers built up.

M.J.

I think about my affair with J. About making love to one of my husband's students. I let these thoughts rise while M and I watch the Johnny Carson show. Johnny is up there on the screen, swinging his imaginary golf club at an imaginary golf ball right into my imaginary love life. Wham! Every night another green-stained Spalding: nicked and worn, pocked and dull, plops into my shallow bed and remains there in the cool: hiding.

a) I do not have a child.

b) I do not have a pet.

c) I do not have a plant.

d) I have ESP. I can read letters without opening them. I can tell colors with my eyes closed. I dream the present and the future. I can tell what M is doing at this very moment. My powers insinuate themselves into other lives.

When M drinks he leaves gifts. Once he left bullets in a neighbor's boots; another time it was a ceramic cat abandoned by him on a New Jersey porch. I used to forgive him everything, thinking it would never happen again, but M can't resist a practical joke: he has actually pulled a rug out from under me, thrown me down in front of oncoming traffic, destroyed an armoire with an ax. Because of the crazy things he has done, we have had to move time and time again. . . . I'm tired ot it . . . tired of barely escaping alive.

M puts two bullets and a note:

IF YOU CHANGE YOUR MIND, THERE MAY
STILL BE TIME!
F. STACY SWARD
NATIONAL RIFLE ASSOCIATION

into a business envelope. He writes the name of a former
colleague on it. The name is Lew Harris. M scrawls the
name across the envelope in big bold script. He is using a
Pentel pen. He runs the letters across the paper with a
mad flourish, as if he is signing a document of great
importance. He goes out. He gets into our station wagon.
He settles in. He drives. He waves to some students he
knows. M stops the car at 98th Street and Riverside
Drive. He gets out. He double-parks. He runs up marble
steps. He scans the doorbells. He takes the crisp envelope
out of his jacket pocket. He shakes the bullets to one side
and holds the thin edge of the envelope as high as the
chrome around the bells reaches. He forces it between the
brick wall and the flat chrome. M returns to the car and
zooms away.

I use the Larry Mathews beauty salon in the Great Northern Hotel. It is on 57th Street between Sixth and Seventh Avenues. The number 5 (Fifth Avenue) bus gets me there. I go all the way down the long lobby and turn right at the glass doors. Inside, I pass the appointment desk, behind which is an aviary of wigs: bloodless beheadings perched on shelves. All around the salon, other women, like me, only uglier, sit in soft cotton print robes (stenciled leopard), giving themselves to the moment of rejuvenation: haircut, shampoo, hair set, pedicure, makeup. And music plays to the soft rustle of off-white curl papers falling to the floor. Everywhere the hypnotic hum of machinery in the service of beauty persists, as if a hypnotist were saying, ". . . you are asleep . . ." Heat blows gently out of tiny vents drilled into transparent hair-drying bubbles; there is a subtle woodwind of sound as manicure tables are rolled across the floor.

The manicurist takes one of my hands and caresses it before using the cuticle clippers. My other hand dips delicately, all tips, all pink asparagus, into a dessert plate of soapy water.

J: shy. Seventeen. He owns a telescope. He mounts it on a tripod; observes the stars above his roof: "If I'm lucky I'll see a comet." He spends hours waiting in the cold to see it. Once it flashed across the sky. Once it did. But it may have been something else.

"J, good-bye." I was crying. He was crying too.

"If you want to know what I think about your not wanting to see me anymore, I think it's mean . . . very mean!" I said. I had a Bloody Mary; he was not allowed to drink.

He was crying too.

"Look," I said, "I can get a key from my girlfriend; she said she'd let me use her place anytime. We don't have to wander around in hallways and parks anymore. We don't have to be afraid that Mark'll come home . . . or that your mother will disturb us."

"You don't understand," he said. "I want you to tell Mark about us. If you love me, you'll tell him. I don't want to hide my love for you anymore. I want you to live with me."

"I can't tell him," I said.

J had been adamant. He withdrew his hand which I had been holding under the table.

◉

I use Le De by Givenchy. So does June Wolff. Strange coincidence: as if I had seduced J by the familiar scent.

Her mouse of a son crawling to me . . . on top of me. "Did you come?" I asked. I should not have sat cheek to cheek with him, looking at Japanese erotica.

No, I was not his first woman. His second. The first was French. His stepfather put her up to it (she was his stepfather's mistress). And she must have taught him very little . . . an apprehensive technique involving the vagina and the clitoris at the same time. He had trouble with his fingers: where should they go?

◉

Two Christmases ago, I had come up out of the snow and stood in the foyer, in front of the shell collection. My face was glowing. J kissed me. And his sister Letitia kissed me. And June kissed me. Letitia gave me a Christmas decoration for a gift: a fragile glass ball painted green, with a nouveau-arte butterfly wrapping its brightly painted wings around the ball. I have it still, wrapped in tissue paper, tucked into a corner of my lingerie drawer. J gave me an antique, hand-carved number puzzle; the numbers were pasted onto thick, movable wooden cubes, and all were contained in a square wooden box. The object of the puzzle is to move the numbers around without taking them out of the box, and to have them read in order from one to fifteen, leaving one empty space in which to maneuver. After J left me, I found myself playing with the puzzle, jumbling the numbers up, dumping them out . . . cheating to get them right.

June gave me a fan that had belonged to Letitia: circa Victoriana. Letitia's room was crowded with things Victorian: Victorian lampshade, Victorian blouse made of lace, reticules, fans, faded silk roses, boxes of horn, a long satin skirt with bustle, and photographs of Diamond Jim Brady, Lillian Russell, Sarah Bernhardt, Oscar Wilde . . . to the photograph of Oscar Wilde she had pasted a nosegay of purple and wine petals (pansies?). It made the photograph seem to be in the process of materializing; but if it actually had, poor Mr. Wilde would have been a basket case, since he had been photographed from the waist up.

I recall that the Christmas ball was not a gift from Letitia. I bought it from her for three dollars and fifty cents. But my gifts to both June and Letitia were antique Victorian enameled pins, each displayed in its own "collector's item" red velvet box.

J received nothing. I stood in front of the window of a Village men's shop and admired him in a transparent posing jock. My weightless, see-through hand held him as he turned away.

I think about dying my hair another color; to become another person, a person who is beautiful, but M warns me against it. He says it would make me look like a whore. I know that M finds whores exciting. . . .

Some of the best-looking people I've ever seen are whores. Although some of them look like Barbie dolls: big blonde wigs, and skinny brown legs hanging out of ass-high miniskirts. Still, it's cute and seems innocent, as if they are playing at being adult. Sweet to see them parading when the weatherman predicts rain: carrying umbrellas, wearing boots, plastic babushkas over elaborate wigs . . . just like Scarsdale matrons.

I was taken for a whore in Riker's one evening. I said, "No" to a drunken salesman. One of the authentic whores, in a red-knit-wool, two-piece, tight dress, had turned to a friend and in a very loud voice said: "He got the right string, but the wrong Yo-Yo."

We sat around the horseshoe counter nursing cups of tea. A pink man with a red neck put his brown-trousered knee against my bare one.

"I have two boats. I'll bet you don't believe me," he said. "Ever been to New Hampshire? I have two boats in New Hampshire. I'll draw you a picture of my boats. Where's a pencil?"

I gave him a pencil.

"Naw, you don't believe me. You don't think I have any boats."

I told him that I had a boat too, made out of paper, and that I floated it in my bathtub.

"I have a bathtub in my room. I'll bet you don't believe I have a bathtub in my room. Wanna come with me to my room?"

"No."

"What's your price? I'm willing to pay."

That question had confused me. As I left the restaurant, I pondered how to price myself, since I had never been sold before.

The man's voice followed me, pleading: "Where you going? Don't leave me alone; I haven't told you about my boats. I have to sell one; I hate to sell it."

⬤

M is walking on the Upper East Side alone. He is nervous. He notices a big black Cadillac following him. He stops walking. It cruises up to him. Stops. There are two women seated in front. One of them propositions him. He is not interested in that one. She is too thin for him. The women change places at the wheel. The full-bodied one is asking him to get in the car. I can see that M is frightened. He wants to walk away. The full-bodied woman gets out of the car. She squats down between M and the car. She urinates. M watches as piss streams out, wetting her legs and hitting the car door before it trickles down the curb. He is almost interested. He asks her price. She tells him. He does not have enough. He is sorry. She gets back in the car: has a conference with the other hooker. They agree to charge him less if he puts it in the window.

"Put it in the window, honey."

Her mouth is open; the window is open.

M imagines his prick being sucked off while the window silently rises to capture him, forcing him to run alongside the car as it picks up speed.

The whores spot a police officer and take off.

⊕

The sign on the gymnasium wall says: NOW THAT YOU'VE DONE YOUR HAIR, WHAT ABOUT YOUR BODY?

Yes, what about it? I want to keep trim so as not to shock J. So far, we have managed to make love under things: my skirt, the sheets, a draped lamp. I know what I look like, but he doesn't, and I daren't let him find out. What M thinks doesn't really concern me anymore. . . . I wouldn't want him wanting me too much . . . not while I'm wanting J. Of course there's the chance that I might be left by both of them! But then, I can always live in my head. What I dream is infinitely better than what I do . . . the hazards far less.

⊕

"Can I help you?" The gymnasium assistant, a slender girl in tights, pressing her false eyelashes down, approaches me.

"I'm just looking," I say.

Four women in black, their desperate flesh in action, lean forward, grab the air, kick in place, shift, speed up, bounce buttocks of overwhelming gravity to the mat. M would be disgusted by their energy. A girl straddles a whirling drum of wooden rollers, quivers sexually, poised for orgasm. Another stands in a stainless-steel skirt on a platform; she leans forward to support herself as tiers of steel springs rub up and down her hips, bruising the fatty tissue hidden under soft gray warm-up pants. This would delight M: her passivity, her acceptance of injury.

"Would you care to see our sauna now?" I follow the attendant. "You may have this visit free, madam. If you care to use the sauna today, we provide you with a towel, slippers, and robe."

I enter the sauna with only a towel wrapped around me. I spread it on an upper wooden bench, breathe deeply, and lie down . . . strung out in body fragrance.

"Do you know that you should not lie there like that," J says to me admiringly. "Do you know that I want to unwrap you as if you were a mysterious package?"

"Yes, unwrap me. Find me." I am partially unwrapped already. I am wearing red nylon French panties: no crotch, ready for action. It is early afternoon. M is away at work.

J says, "The existence of another planet-like body outside our solar system has been deduced from observations made at the Sproul Observatory at Swarthmore College in Pennsylvania."

"Really?"

"It took scientists thirty years to find it. Its mass is greater than Jupiter, the largest planet in the solar system!"

"Time solves everything," I say. "I guess if those scientists keep looking through their telescopes, they'll see backward to the beginning of time. Is that possible? Is it possible to see something that doesn't exist anymore?"

J says, "I don't know about seeing it, but some astronomers believe that they've picked up short waves: sounds of the beginning of the earth, of creation . . . it's part of the 'big bang' theory."

"I have a 'big bang' theory myself," I say. "Let's go into the bedroom and I'll demonstrate."

I take him by the hand, I always take him by the hand, he is a child: afraid to go, afraid to stay.

First we play tent: both under the sheet, my legs in the air form a central pole. The soft and powdery, white-blueness of the sheet seems made of congealed water. The interior warmth of our enclosed dome is forty to eighty degrees higher than the atmosphere prevailing outside.

A tiny red light illuminates a corner of the sauna.

Another time: J stands in the doorway, afraid to come in. He thinks of the bed as M's bed. I initiate a game to bring him to me. "I'll bet I know something you won't do," I say.

"No, you don't," J answers hopefully.

"Ah, yes, I do," I say. J responds to the challenge. He is ready to do anything I ask.

"What do you know that I won't do?" he asks again.

"I'll bet you won't kiss me here."

He flutters around my muslin cage. The mouth of the moth cannot resist the light of my mercury lamp: an additional tease. My sex extends over several acres . . . he cannot escape me. He puts his tongue in: licks my fur.

"You won't do it!" I repeat over, and over, and over, and over, and over, and over. . . .

"Let me see what happens to my penis when it's in you?" he asks, putting two fingers into my vagina. I press and release my muscles, feigning orgasm. He mounts me . . . enters me . . . centers me . . . his penis doing a better job than his fingers in obtaining and recording woman information: it wants to do the exploration itself. To make this possible for him, I provide maximum safety: I call to him, "Oh, J, I love you . . . !" I am a stepping-stone into grown-up territory.

His mouth cruelly sucks the very life-spit out of my mouth, out of my mound, out of my mind . . .

I come.

○

If only we had a place of our own.

○

Lew Harris and his wife are on their way to see a movie. He wants to see *Vixen*, she wants to see *The Sound of Music*. They are arguing. They spot the envelope that M left for Lew Harris.

"Look, darling, it has your name on it." Mrs. Harris takes it down. She expects to read something very nice.

They read the note, rush right back upstairs, and call the police. Lew Harris is racking his brain to think of who his enemy might be. He decides that he has no enemies. He cannot recall ever having signed a petition to initiate better gun control laws. He is rereading the note: IF YOU CHANGE YOUR MIND, THERE MAY STILL BE TIME!

30

"I'm willing to change my mind," he says helplessly, "but about what?"

He decides that the note could not have been written by a member of the National Rifle Association, because a threatening note would only hurt their cause. He barely handles the bullets; they frighten him. He imagines the size hole they'd leave in him . . . the blood that would pour out! He is trying not to panic. He looks nervously out the windows of his apartment to see if anyone is staked out on the adjoining roofs.

The police arrive. One of them requests the letter. On reading it carefully, he says, "Well it don't actually say 'this bullet's got your name on it.' It would be different if the person who wrote this letter to you had one a them bullets pegged for you. . . . I mean, this ain't necessarily a threatenin' letter."

"But the bullets themselves . . ." Lew Harris says, "don't you think the bullets are threatening? Don't you think they mean something in relation to the note?"

The policeman reads the note again. "Nope, this is probably the work of a crank. Don't mean a thing. Anyway, there's nothing we can do about it, unless the guy actually shoots you."

"You mean there's really nothing you can do to prevent something happening?" Lew Harris is not willing to wait until he is shot before the law goes into action.

The cop says: "We could call the detective down at our precinct, have the name and handwriting checked out to see if we have a file on this guy . . . see if he's been using the mails for this purpose."

Harris, desperate, says, "It wasn't sent through the mails; it was delivered by hand and left by the bells downstairs."

The cop ponders this as he observes, with obvious disapproval, a nude sketch hanging on the wall. "I can't see that there's been a violation, but tell you what . . . I'll call Detective Mulholland and see what he has to say."

"Thank you very much." Lew Harris is hoping that Detective Mulholland will put on an around-the-clock guard. He mentions it to the cop.

The cop says, "We ain't got a force big enough to handle this kind of thing. It would be different if you was a celebrity . . . but you're just John Doe, average citizen. You realize, sir, that if a mentally deranged person wants to get you, he'll find a way, no matter how well guarded you are?"

"I know," Lew Harris answers.

"Can you think of anyone who might want to harm you?"

"I've gone through all the possibilities, and there's no one."

The other cop reports his phone conversation with Detective Mulholland. "He says we should take the evidence down to the station house and he'll check it out. He'll call you in a few days if anything turns up;

32

meanwhile, if you find something out yourself, you can get in touch with him."

They leave with the envelope which contains the bullets and M's unsettling communication.

◉

"I don't know what to do," Lew Harris says, wondering whether he and his wife ought to make another foray in the direction of the movies.

"Do? Let's get the hell out of New York!" she answers him.

"I won't allow myself to be terrorized . . . no . . . I've got to find out who's playing this horrible joke on us."

"Could it have been one of your students?" Mrs. Harris suggests.

"Couldn't be; I'm the one defends them against the other teachers."

Lew Harris's wife is thinking that if she leaves the house with him she becomes a moving target. She decides not to be seen with him. She makes him a cup of tea and they sit smiling across the table at each other.

It occurs to Lew Harris that his enemy might be M! M, who speaks about hunting, who passionately defends the right of every U.S. citizen to own guns . . . "He's the only one I know with guns," Lew Harris explains to his wife, "and just last week I intervened for a kid, a Charles Thomas whom he was picking on. It made him furious. He passed a remark about how the kid deserved to be shot . . . and I said, nobody deserves to get shot! Besides, a gun is to kill! And he said: 'You don't have to kill with a gun, you can scare with it.' That's all I said, a gun is to kill. But I can't just come right out and accuse him. . . . Besides, would he admit it?"

⬤

I don't usually kiss photographs. But J is standing against a green girder in the subway FIFTH AVENUE stop. It is a color photo: pink face, blue work shirt open at the neck, dark-blue pants. A camera in a leather camera case hangs from his neck. He has a hand over the camera to steady it. The other hand is in his pocket. A red gum machine shields us from the eyes of transit passengers waiting for the train. I kiss J on his melancholy, glossy lips; I smooth his hair back with my pinky.

The way J looks at Letitia: is it envy or lust? Does he want to be her, or be in her? We watched her making pomander balls for Christmas, stabbing the swollen fruit with spiked cloves until the aromatic pome resembled a mace. J winced.

"Won't they rot?" I asked.

"No, they dry out and become fragrant. I hang them in the closet and put them in my drawers. People used to carry them around to guard against infection."

"Why don't you carry one around; see if it works," I said.

"I'm already infected," Letitia answered.

J . . . I'll bet you slept with your sister . . . remember, on Christmas Day Letitia was ill . . . a urinary infection . . . I had had the very same thing the week before, and I had slept with you, not knowing I had it . . . it is highly contagious. Did you pass it on to Letitia? Did you sleep with her? She has a habit of sprawling when she sits . . . and I noticed a box of birth control pills on her night table. June is much too liberal with you guys.

FRAME UP!

I, Charles Thomas, on November 7, 1969, during the first period, was proceeding to Driver's Education class in the West Tower; to get there I had to walk through the big gym. The gym teacher, Mr. Mark Johnson, was holding a class, and physically prevented me from going to class by standing in front of the door. He said: "You can't go through." When I insisted, "Would you please let me through because this is my first day back in school, and I have missed a lot of work," he asked, "What's your name (boy)?" And I said, "Puddin' Tain, ask me again and I'll tell you the same." Then I said, "It looks like you and me are going to stand here for the rest of the period." He said, "I guess so, because I have nothing else to do." I then called him a "mother," and pushed past him. And ran. I finally reached Driver's Ed., I won't tell you how. Toward the end of the period, Mr. Johnson walked into the room, pointed at me, and said, "I want that boy's name." At the end of the first period I went down to his office, took the piece of paper with my name and official class on it out of his hand and tore it up, and said: "If you want to get me in trouble, get me in trouble on your own time, not mine!" I walked out of his office, and on to my second-period class.

On November 7, I was automatically suspended from

school, because the administration had stated that I threatened Mr. Johnson's life. You, my fellow students, know that Mr. Johnson is a sadist, and has been known to kick, put his foot on students' necks when they are down, twist arms behind backs, and otherwise harass scapegoats during gym period. But I was also accused of "insubordination," harassment of teachers and students, being detrimental to the social welfare of the population of our school, and all in all, a dangerous student! I was never given a preliminary school hearing, was suspended from participation in all school events, and received a special-delivery, certified-mail letter on November 16 from the Board of Education, at 110 Livingston Street, office of high schools, that a suspension hearing would be held there November 25, at 10 A.M., room 730B . . .

Support Charles! Come to his hearing! There are Board of Education directives preventing this kind of action. We cannot allow the administration to exercise arbitrary, unjust, and illegal punishment to remove students they dislike from the schools!

Charles Thomas appears to me in the foyer, to the left of the umbrella stand. He is pale. His natural chocolate color faded. I gaze at him awhile before speaking.

37

"I want to thank you for standing up to my husband. Now there are two of us who know the true story . . . look!"

I bare my chest on which there still remains a large footprint. It is ingrained. Charles Thomas gives me a jar of bleaching cream and a piece of #00 sandpaper.

"You gonna look like a piece of raw meat for a few weeks," Charles Thomas says, "but after that you gonna have skin as fine as a baby's ass."

"Are you coming back to see me?"

"I'll be around. . . ."

My evocation of Charles Thomas lasts only a short time; and I am alone again, in the present. M puts his finger on the bell, ringing it without stopping. He does it to bother me, hoping that I am as far away from the door as possible, so that I will have to come running.

"Why don't you open the door with your key?" I demand.

"My hands were full," he says, putting down his briefcase, a pile of newspapers, magazines, letters, flag stickers, old underwear, gloves, and the neighbor's garbage. We look at each other; there is nothing left but vexations. I remember when he used to call me his "darling little invalid"; watched for signs of illness so he could take care of me . . . draw out my fever.

"What did you do today?" he says accusingly.

"Nothing much." I keep from him the information that I have read Charles Thomas's FRAME UP! and managed to meet him soon afterward . . . that we achieved an instant rapport verging on friendship.

"Get busy and make me a snack," he orders. I bring him a quart of milk and a box of Social Tea crackers. He gulps down all the milk and finishes the box of crackers. He is not as active as he used to be, but still has a "jock's" appetite. He goes to sleep after eating. I wonder whether the Board of Education will actually prevent Charles Thomas from continuing his education . . . whether they will give him a fair hearing.

M puts the basketballs away in the storage closet. He locks the door. He goes into the gym office. A dark-green shade covers the small window in the door. He takes a handful of Dixon Ticonderoga Leadfast pencils out of a new box and sharpens each one by pressing it into the electric sharpener.

A buzz of carnal delight zings through him as the pencils, being eaten alive in the machine, grow smaller and sharper. He would like to put his finger in, his nose, or something else. He admires the cold efficiency of its function.

Lew Harris bursts into M's room. He grabs him, shakes him, shouts, "Did you leave an envelope with two bullets in it, for me? Did you?"

"I might have," M gasps.

"Did you?" Lew Harris shoves him against his desk. A can of crayons falls to the floor, spilling its contents. M tries to twist away to pick up the crayons. The school bell rings. It is out of order. It keeps ringing. The sound startles Lew Harris. He lets M go. M grovels on his hands and knees, searching for crayons, paper clips, marbles.

"What do you mean, you might have!"

"It's entirely possible. I've done that kind of thing before."

"Think! Did you or didn't you? Admit it . . . you did write that note to me, didn't you! My wife is very sick about it; she refuses to leave the house. And you cost me a screw last night too!"

M is up. He slowly turns toward Lew Harris. He says, "I admit it, but it was only a joke. I thought you'd recognize my handwriting. I meant no harm."

"Recognize your handwriting?! Man, I wouldn't recognize my own handwriting. I don't know what to do about you, I really don't."

M sweats profusely. He is experiencing the same sense of danger he had felt when, as a youth, he had gone down the steps to the basement of his home after an argument with his father, taken a double-barreled shotgun from the rack, loaded both chambers, put the barrel against his forehead just above the eyebrows, and . . . not tripped the triggers.

M says, "Have you gone to the police?"

"What do you think? They have your letter and your bullets."

"But they don't know it was me, do they? They don't know about me?" M pleads.

"Not yet."

"Please don't give them my name . . . they'll bother us . . . my wife and I . . . they'll make it tough! Look, I haven't kept the guns; my mother has them locked up. I do this every once in a while when I drink. I promise I won't drink anymore . . . ever."

Sick to his stomach, Lew Harris turns swiftly and leaves.

I ask M to write a letter of apology to Mrs. Harris. He says he will. But he insists that I deliver it by hand along with a conciliatory gift: *History of Art* by H. W. Janson. The Harrises are interested in art.

Dear Mrs. Harris,

When a man behaves like a jackass, as I have done however inadvertently, he does not escape easily from his own censures—nor will I. The details of the full extent of my lunacy involved the distribution of a box of rifle shells, the destruction of a television set, running at ninety miles an hour across the Jersey countryside with a sounding horn for company, and several other aberrations too shameful to mention to a stranger.

That you were in any way upset by my crude and vulgar foolishness is something I am heartily sorry for. Please believe there was neither malice nor intent in the action—only some stupid alcoholic fantasy which I deeply regret affected your life and that of others.

Will you please accept my apologies which I hope, in part, can replace the pain my heedless actions may have caused?

Sincerely,
Mark Johnson

M has gone to the Pokerino Palace, where he can be surrounded by extravagant gifts: lawn croquet group, electric blanket, shotgun, Early American lamp, hi-fi, sterling silver platter . . . he is trying to add up winning points . . . he needs 1,500 more tickets. I used to go with him, before he became so obsessive. The cheap stuff palled on him: the pocket combs, finger traps, miniature cards, nail clippers, and dice, that I still get a kick out of. M is a much better player than I am. He knows where he wants the ball to roll, and it obeys him. He's had a flush, a royal flush, a straight, and full house many times. He considers it a waste of a nickel when I get my three of a kind . . . treats Pokerino as if it were an Olympic event. Oh, I know it's pretty stupid to sit glued to a stool watching rubber balls roll into holes on a slanted board . . . yet it was something we had together. Once when we were totally engrossed in the game (and a radio was playing over the loudspeaker), the program was interrupted by the announcer who said: "LADIES AND GENTLEMEN, YOUR NATIONAL ANTHEM!" M and I jumped up and stood at attention, our hands over our hearts, our stools spinning free. And there wasn't even a flag present. It broke us up! The evening was one to remember.

I have a signal that lets J know when I want to see him. I allow the phone two rings, then hang up. As soon as M leaves for Pokerino I dial J's number. This time I wait for him to pick up . . . I long to hear his voice.

"Hello," I say, "this is Melissa."

"How are you?" J asks. He sounds as if he is speaking to someone he barely knows. Perhaps this is because June is around. Most probably it is because I refuse to bring our affair into the open. J is preparing himself for a break. He is obstinate as a child. He is a child after all, and wants things his way . . . or not at all. But if we separate (like the white from the yolk of an egg), some of me will cling to him always.

"What are you doing?" I hope he is doing nothing.

"I was trying out the tape recorder June got me. I don't like the sound of my voice."

"I like the sound of your voice. Wanna come over?"

"You're crazy if you like my voice . . . it's so monotonous. I'm sorry June bought me the tape recorder, maybe she can give it back."

"Bring it over with you, darling, I'll buy it. But hurry, and don't be sad. Don't be alone, I love you."

J has placed the tape recorder on the table. It can feel the magnetic pull of love emanating from us with equal power. That is why it does not slide in either direction, but remains fastened. It is a small cassette-type machine, simple to operate. In order to record, two buttons must be pushed down simultaneously. I do this and we are ready. The tape makes tiny whirring sounds, like a captured fly grown tired trying to escape.

"What shall we talk about?" J asks.

"Tell me what you're afraid of," I answer.

"No."

I hear J draw in a quick slippery breath. Saliva bubbles at the corners of his mouth. I expect him to spit. Instead he swallows.

"Then let's make love," I suggest.

"No . . . I don't want to anymore."

"Why did you come over?"

"Because you asked me to," he says.

After J leaves, I find a magazine on the closet floor. It is called *Jr.* and features photos of young men in posing briefs, leather, or jeans. It must have dropped from J's coat pocket.

The tape recorder is on. I am J's voice. I am also his male lover. By creating a situation, I hope to read J's mind. . . . He is afraid that he is homosexual. This is not in keeping with the rest of his generation who claim to harbor no guilt.

J's lover has him tied, facedown on the bed. J is nude. His firm buttocks have a beautiful freshness, almost female in their rising plumpness. His lover says:

"How delightful to touch and squeeze your bum!"

J twists and turns trying to loosen his bonds. The other, armed with a magnificent cock, commences to deflower him. The delicate hole of pleasure, a chrysanthemum violated, receives three or four thrusts of fullest length. J sustains the insertion with cries of joy. His lover's stones slap against his raised buttocks.

J   Oh, I am overcome with voluptuous sensations.
Lover   I distill my very soul into you.
J   Bury yourself in me.
Lover   Ah!
J   Pleasure suffocates me.
Lover   Come! Come!
J   Beastly, unnatural! Oh, save me, Father!

So, it is true!

J says, "Mummy should have a boyfriend."

"Yes, J, how about you?"

We are at a party at June's house. J is afraid to go out. He climbs into June's bed. He curls up in the fetal position. He says, "I'm going to sleep with you, Mummy. I'm never getting out of your bed." I say, "Make him get out immediately."

We both have to carry him into the living room; we seat him on the couch. His eyes glisten with tears. He does not say a word. The party is over.

I am startled by the news that you want to kill yourself. That you ran screaming into the street: past the Nedicks, past the subway, around the corner and past the flower shop, the menswear store, the cleaners, the Maritime Building, across Greenwich Avenue where you hoped you would be run over by a truck and killed! Yet

June caught you in front of the toy store . . . and took you home again. Now she's afraid to leave you alone.

◉

June says: "J asked me, 'What is a tragedy?'"

◉

J, listen to me child . . . M is a terrible lover . . . he is no lover at all. He has to tie me to the bed and pretend he is ravishing a virgin. It is a bore. I can tell you this because you are having a breakdown and don't know what I'm saying anyway. When you and I were together, J, I never spoke of M in a disparaging way, did I? I always said, "I'd hate to hurt Mark." Didn't I?

◉

Semiannual party: fiesta time at your high school. J, you are wearing a black suit, white shirt, and a gray, green, and pink diagonally striped tie. You are small.

You are beautiful. Your hands are unusually large though. I am thought to be a relative of yours when I ask where you are. You are in a big room, helping with the fiesta food: paella, pastillelios, pasacaglia, pastiche, pirogen, and pistachio nuts. Your classmates are dancing . . . you are with the over-thirties. I wonder why you never learned to dance? I see you looking at young girls' legs. I am jealous. I shouldn't be; I should be happy for you; I should be worried that you are not like the other boys. Your difference is a symptom, and I weep for you, child.

There must be something about me that attracts unhappy people. I hope I don't lose all of them.

It is freezing out. J and I go into a coffee shop. There is a minimum of twenty-five cents per person. I have the money for the coffee. J has only enough for carfare. We put our hands together to see how small mine are compared to his. I close my eyes and let touch take over. It is one of the most exciting moments of my life.

When I walk with M, he becomes enraged if I show interest in a passing male. He hits me on the head with his newspaper. It makes a hollow popping sound and embarrasses me. He thinks I am getting hot for a stranger . . . a younger, thinner, bouncier stranger . . . but always I am projecting an image of J. It is not young men I love. It is J, and always will be J. In twenty years J will be thirty-nine. In twenty years, I will be . . . ?

M says that Charles Thomas has discovered that he is a foster child . . . and doesn't like it! That he has become a menace.

110 Livingston Street. The board waited one and a half hours for Charles Thomas to appear. He did not. Students have taken over the lunchroom in protest against his unjust suspension. Fliers from the principal circulate:

To All Students:

It is important that you as students know what actually took place in the negotiations between the student negotiating team and the administration. The principal had *already agreed* to the following demands when the negotiations broke down because of the insistence upon the part of the students that total amnesty be granted for any future actions as a condition for any further talks.

Agreed:

1. The concept of a student court to replace the principal's suspension.

2. The reopening of the hearing for Charles Thomas and a letter from the principal to the superintendent who has final authority in the case, urging reinstatement of Charles provided he can give assurance of proper behavior.

3. Total amnesty for yesterday's and today's actions.

NOTE: I will still abide by these decisions despite the breakdown of talks, and I am willing to resume talks on the remainder of the demands at any time.

Gordon B. Choate
Principal

Mrs. Harris does not want to let me in. Lew Harris opens the door. I come in with the letter for Mrs. Harris, and the art history book. She is looking at me with repugnance.

"Mark wants you to have this book and this letter," I say, putting them on the table. Mrs. Harris does not even open the letter. She picks it up by the corner and drops it into a straw basket.

"I'm sorry," she says, "but I can't accept the book. You'll have to take it back."

"You must keep the book. . . . Mark wants you to have it."

"It gives me the creeps!" she answers. "I don't want it in my house."

"If you don't take it, I'll have to throw it into a garbage can when I go down. . . . I don't dare take it back."

"Suit yourself," she says coldly.

I flip the pages, trying to interest her in its illustrations . . . its desirability, "Look," I say, "celestial drama above a vast Alpine landscape . . . the Diety . . . coquettish damsels whose wriggly nakedness . . . The Kaisersaal . . . Tomb of the Countess . . . mother and child . . . isn't it wonderful! . . . The condensation of centuries under one cover. Please keep it!"

"Your husband belongs in an asylum!" she shouts.

I sit there looking glum. Lew Harris throws a withering glance her way. "Don't tell Mark what she said, he's liable to snap," Harris says. "We'll keep the book . . . tell your husband 'thank you.' "

Charles Thomas has a better body than J.

Charles Thomas has absorbed all color into his skin. He reflects nothing. He contains everything.

J is the absence of color. He reflects my image. He keeps nothing.

I am going to introduce them and change the course of history: hues are produced by blending the three primary colors in various proportions. Adding white to them gives us tints, while mixing them with black produces shades.

J tried to drown himself. June showed me the note:

Dear Mummy,
    My instructions were to self-destruct at zero hour, in order to be born again. And since zero is a

very personal number, the instructor left it up to me, when. I consulted my *Wonder Book of Ocean-ography* in order to find out what lies on the bottom of the sea, because at that depth, all traces of my former fictional self might easily disappear into the mouths of sea beasts. Please believe that I will be happy to disappear into the digestive system of a sea anemone, to become part of that beautiful sprawling flower below the continental slope.

Though the continental slope is just plain mud, Mummy: blue mud, green mud, red mud, black mud, or white mud, it oozes over billions of tiny shells and skeletons of creatures which, like myself, have lived near the surface of the sea, and then upon death have drifted downward to the very bottom. Good-bye. Don't fret.

J

June lets the water out of the tub. She demands that J never fall asleep in the tub again. He goes back to polishing a telescope lens he has made. It takes hours. What does he think while he is polishing?

"I'm not thinking anything," he says.

I realize now that his arrogant posture is due to an internal conflict in him between loving and fleeing. I assume that he is attracted by, and afraid of me. His courtship consists in part in running away from me. I will not call again and ask for him.

⊕

June is, in spirit, a female phalarope. When she was pregnant she would have preferred having the male of the species incubate and guard the young alone. She is not interested in the traditional motherly chores.

⊕

M and I are on our way to the library. We are stopped by a reporter and a photographer who want to ask us a question. They are from a well-known morning paper. M says, "Shoot . . . what's the question?"

THE QUESTION
    If you were on a sinking ship, and could save only one other person, your spouse or your child, who would you choose?

WHERE ASKED
    Along Amsterdam Avenue.

THE ANSWERS
Mark Johnson, teacher:

I would have to try to save the child. A child hasn't lived yet, but an adult has in most instances tasted everything and is just marking time here on earth. Also, a child depends entirely on an adult, and it is the honorable thing to do, to live up to this trust. Besides, my wife is an excellent swimmer and could probably save both of us.

Melissa S. Johnson, housewife:

My child. If I allowed my child to die, I could not go on living myself. My husband is an excellent swimmer and could probably save all of us.

◉

I have never learned to swim. Does this mean that my hypothetical child is doomed?

◉

M, you are covered with patriotic gore . . . it won't come out at the cleaners. I asked you to take it in long before the fabric rotted, but you just lay on the bed, waiting for soft white veins of plaster to open and sift down over you. You spent one entire year gazing at the ceiling . . . and you blamed it on the "Commies"!

⊛

A young photographer said: "I was in Vietnam taking pictures, stumbled on a hospital in the hills: one thousand children under twelve with varying degrees of burns over their bodies and limbs. Many of them were crying; many of them were dying. I have to shut myself off. Can't take the emotion. I concentrate on composing the picture. You know it isn't so bad when the napalm hits you straight on, because then you're gone and don't know what happened. The terrible thing is when a few drops get you . . ."

The pictures are going to be published in a book. I asked the photographer to let me know when it comes out. I'm going to give it to M as a birthday present. He doesn't want to bring the boys back.

⊛

"Charles Thomas," I say, "maybe we can help some black people together . . . not here in New York, of course . . . not even in Chicago or Connecticut . . ."

"I don't have nothing to say to you, baby," he says.

"Don't you want to get even with Mr. Johnson for having you suspended?"

"He don't figure. I got bigger plans. I goin' to burn the school down . . . if he in it, that too bad!"

M's beard should be highly inflammable; after he brushes it each morning, he uses my hair spray which is a highly inflammable lacquer.

Charles Thomas feels so good he sings me a song:

> "Burn, baby, burn
> there's something you must learn
> when the fat is in the fire
> whitey stokes the funeral pyre
> when the flames are jumping higher
> white turns black as he expire
> Burn, baby, burn
> there's something you must learn
> when the shit is in the tree
> that's the place the panther be
> when the shit is on the ground
> whitey ain't goin' be around
> So, burn, baby, burn!"

I compliment Charles on his excellent singing voice . . . ask him again to accompany me on a goodwill tour. Again he refuses . . . so . . . I decide to shanghai him. I need him, I need him! And I have to help somebody, and somebody have to help me.

I slip into the cafeteria where there is still a sit-in going on. The steam table is steaming: hot vegetables, meat loaf, halibut sauce diablo, soup de jour. I am wearing a white apron, hair in a net, and white sneakers; a flowered handkerchief is pinned to the breast pocket of my uniform. I am mistaken for a cafeteria worker. Nobody else is allowed in.

In this guise I concoct a Mickey Finn consisting of:

> 3 crushed onions (essence)
> 4 cloves of garlic (chopped)
> 1 tsp. lemon extract (undiluted)
> 8 ounces warm milk (whole)
> 5 tbs. honey
> Cinnamon (1 stick)
> 6 ounces of paregoric

I serve it to Charles Thomas who belts it down without a second's hesitation. He turns blue. He passes out behind a rack of aluminum trays. We extricate ourselves, me mumbling, "Emergency, emergency . . ." and are helped into the elevator, then out into a cab (where he vomits into the declivity between my breasts).

We go to Biafra . . . directly . . . flying inconspicuously above the clouds. I snore, so that Charles Thomas will believe we are in an airplane.

Can we stem the tide of human suffering?

✱

WE ATTEMPT TO STEM THE TIDE
OF HUMAN SUFFERING (*anyway*)

I am almost a nurse. Charles Thomas is almost a
doctor. We are wearing white, and we care. We are
holding the first medical clinic here (Chuba, Biafra [Ni-
geria]) in twenty-seven months of war, amid people
suffering from protein starvation and resembling inmates
of a concentration camp: which they are, even though
they spend as much time outdoors as in.

These people are refugees.

We are tourists.

They say that when they reached the deserted farm
settlement here, near the Niger River, it seemed a
"Garden of Paradise."

"Oh, yes, Mis-tah! Rich cassava grow by himself on
many miles of farmland and in the bush."

"Then what happened?" I ask, kneeling on the floor
beside a sick child. I feel his swollen belly and stalk-thin,
chocolate-colored limbs pocked with white scabs. Charles

Thomas continues interpreting for me as I prescribe drip feed for the child, and press diuretic pills into the hand of his anxious mother.

"Tell her it is necessary for the child to take them in order to relieve the pressure of urine blocked inside."

The child will die (anyway).

His mother whispers more information about the "Garden of Paradise." "We were so thirsty, but the well was sick, Mis-tah! We sneak the drink an' get dysentry . . . yes."

WE WAIT FOR HELP (anyway)

Charles and I are desperate, but we are healthy . . . we have to keep saying to ourselves: "If we were sick we couldn't help." Our physical affluence is obscene: the flesh too firm, the eyes too clear, the limbs too steady. But if we were sick ourselves, how could we be of assistance?

We have sent seventeen children to the hospital run by the French Red Cross at Santana, next to Avo-Omama . . . we hear that only two survived.

Outside, the sound of a thousand people murmuring and grunting like fallen birds with a snoutful of pain; they wait for our help (anyway).

Charles Thomas turns to me imploringly. "I may have to beat up some of them to keep them in line," he says.

We pass among them, choosing who will enter the clinic. We hand out precious pink clinic cards and wish

61

they were made of rice paper so that the hungry might eat them. The separate lines of children, adults, and very old people press forward whenever a patient hobbles toward the dirty concrete clinic building . . . where we portion out what we have.

I have to fight an impulse to carry the little boys who use canes to walk. I hear a child, with swollen, light-yellow testicles, explain to Charles Thomas: "It hurts to walk, Mis-tah!"

A woman carries in a man on her back, and Charles Thomas whispers to me, "He is dead."

Because it is war, a Nigerian shell lands.

It demolishes a mud-walled house, and injures a number of people. The ones outside the clinic, who have been standing for three hours in the withering sun, scatter into the bush . . . many merely put their eating dish over their heads.

Charles Thomas says, "Man, lookit what's happenin' here, and people are calm! Let's go back and shake 'em up."

I see and hear on the one o'clock news that genocide is an accepted technique of war—from one of its generals!

I go to sleep (anyway).

Why do I invent deaths for those I am attracted to?

I have not invented their deaths. J is suicidal. Charles Thomas is in constant danger because of his skin. There are other hazards: air pollution, the decay of algae in lakes, air traffic, the bomb, all bombs, wars, the war, the next war, disease, dissent, distrust, disgust, dissolution, disappearance. . . . I live close to the highway, I hear cars screeching to a stop every day, avoiding an accident. Sometimes I hear the crash of an accident. When traffic is moving along without incident, it sounds like the ocean.

What do you mean?

I mean I love the sound of the ocean even though it is the sound of heavy rubber tires turning. It helps me to dream.

Tell me what you dream.

For a week before my operation to untip a tipped womb, I had been eating nothing but peanut butter. I couldn't resist it. I was lying on my bed looking up when suddenly I found myself in a twilight state . . . neither conscious, nor unconscious . . . and I felt a miraculous lightness. I had actually left my body; my spirit was hovering over it looking down. I thought, "Isn't this marvelous." Then I heard footsteps in the other room. They terrified me. I was afraid I would not be able to get back into my body in time. Somehow I managed to do it, and gathering myself into a tight human ball I fell asleep at the foot of the bed. Then I dreamt. In the dream I was falling into the ocean. I was not drowning, just falling. . . . I had the thought that falling was the same as rising . . . that the fish in the ocean were the same as the birds in the sky . . . that up was down, and down was up. . . . I became ecstatic and woke up in this state.

Are you fearful of relinquishing the hold you have on reality?

Yes, that is true.

⬤

I go to the park to hang on to life. The grass and trees are green (in part), and this mostly green is real. Children are playing. The sun is shining. My spirit absorbs the rays of the sun, and produces not flowers, but lethargy. I watch the children playing, and wonder what my own child would look like if I had one. At once, all the children have J's face. Their laughter, their shouts, bombard my psyche like a multiwave oscillator, which is a quack's cure-all for mankind.

J, you have warm, wet lips: an unusual hydrothermal experience. Your genitals are like the sego lily: three-petaled, curved, and fragrant, not far from Point Sublime. I expect to travel there again sometime.

J has become Prince Motoyoshi; his poem to me reads:

> Wabi mureba
> Ima hata onaji
> Naniwa haru
> Mi wo tsukushite mo
> Awamu to zo omou

He will not translate it for me. But from it I surmise that he is lonely, doesn't care what happens to him, has to see me, even though it means that he will be lost in Naniwa Bay, because he has a small boat.

I answer his poem in uncertain meter, probably Sapphic. Half of the words come from a found fragment; only the last few words of each line remain. . . . I will put a word in front of each sentence to see if it gives added meaning to the line.

Fuck . . . passion yes.
Fuck . . . utterly.
Fuck . . . I can.
Fuck . . . shall be to me.
Fuck . . . a face.
Fuck . . . shining back at me.
Fuck . . . beautiful.
Fuck . . . indelibly.

I'm sure that J will love it and stop being lonely when he reads it. It is so appreciative of all he's done for me.

J you must never go to sea in a sieve!

M suspects that I am having an affair with J. He is too late; it is almost over. He broods about having been in school all day, not having been able to track me down. Now he is on his way to June's house . . . to catch us. June has flown to Puerto Rico to visit friends who live near the rain forest, so J is alone in the house. He opens the door a crack and turns ashen when he sees M. M asks for me. J says that he is alone and that June is in Puerto Rico. He invites M in. He serves M some of June's pâté, which she left for J to eat while she is gone. He also brings out a bottle of beer and a box of crackers. J pets his cat. M eats out of nervousness. He dips the crackers into the pâté: they break . . . he cannot manage their crisp frailty.

"Well, if Mrs. Johnson happens to drop by, tell her I'm looking for her, will you?" M thinks he is setting a trap.

"I don't expect anybody," J says.

"She said she might come here . . ." M watches for a revealing sign.

"Maybe she doesn't know that June's gone already," J says.

"Maybe she does and maybe she doesn't." M tries to picture J in bed with me . . . it makes him ill . . . he'd prefer being cuckolded by a star athlete, one of his choice.

J locks the door after M leaves, wondering what he wanted.

I take J to the Planetarium. I am a member of the Museum of Natural History and can get in free with one guest. Before we go in to see the show, we step on various scales to see what we would weigh on the moon and other planets. Inside, we sit in the dark, looking up. The man at the heavenly console is lecturing about "What Lies

Beyond Saturn's Rings?" He says that Saturn consists of a molten core surrounded by an ice cover thousands of miles thick.

I put J's hand under my skirt. The Planetarium is the best place to take a date: the darkest. We enter the atmosphere filled with deadly methane and ammonia gases.

"However, this atmosphere is much more stable than Jupiter's," the man says.

My surface temperature rises to about—240 F. Like Jupiter, J makes me rotate quickly. I think that if he and I ever had children, we would name them Phoebe, Hyperion, Mimas, Engladas, Tethys, Diana, Rhea, Iapetus, and Titan. One of them would be different than all the rest (like J); the others would be normal. At breakfast we would always eat half a grapefruit placed facedown in the plate to resemble the top half of Saturn above its rings.

M is euphoric. He has been sent two tickets to a football game at Yale.

"I didn't know they play football in the summertime," I say. He ignores the remark. "I don't want to go with you," I add.

"Good!" he says. "I can sell your ticket for at least seventy-five dollars. I sent for these, but I didn't expect to get them. What a lucky break!"

Charles Thomas is out of the state, ostensibly to organize other Third World students at other high schools, and to help them recognize the hypocrisy of the educational system. He says, "Power . . . then peace!" He has a second, secret identity: "The Tongue." He has always had a powerful tongue. He writes me about his latest campaign to unsettle the establishment, especially rightest white co-eds:

Hi, chiclet,
Seem that at least one UCSH co-ed is fallen prey to "The Tongue." That me, baby. They describe me as a sex-crazed monster who hangs out in the vicinity of the campus lagoon. Well, I was there one 2:45 A.M., one night recently, and I did claim to possess a knife, and the chick did put me down, so I jump in front of her and put my hand over her mouth to stop her from screaming, dig? I say to her, "I got a knife and I won't use it if you cooperate. I won't rape you, just eat you." She was all shook up and didn't give me no back talk, so I dragged her into the bushes and perform cunnilingus on her. Then I apologized and told her that I didn't really

69

have no shiv, and weren't going to cut her. She were so grateful for what I done for her that she give a wrong description to the authorities: white male, six feet, one inch tall, with blond hair and blue eyes. Hair medium length. Wearing a sport jacket, tan pants, no tie. About 23 years of age. They lookin' for that unsavory character right now!

Be a good girl, or the boogie man gonna get you if you don't watch out.

Charles

June once said to me: "If you didn't want to be with M, you wouldn't be. You are not forced to stay with him."

Of course she's right.

But am I with him?

"What is the greatest sin you've ever committed?" I ask M.

He says, "I killed my father and slept with my mother."

M is never serious.

There is a school vacation and I have to leave Charles Thomas and J to go to Yellowstone National Park with M. He is going especially to see our national symbol, the bald eagle, and has written the names of Madison, Firehole, and Yellowstone rivers down; they are places where the bird, recognized by its white tail and head, may occasionally be seen. M is going to take pictures of the bald eagle, and have them blown up to poster size for his den. I don't know how he'll keep from wanting to take potshots at the wall, once it becomes symbolic not only of our country, but of an unbridled energy and strength . . . a free spirit which happens to be on the verge of extinction.

Predator? Yes, the bald eagle is: possessing size, strength, powerful flight, and keenness of vision. We must do all we can to let the bald eagle live . . . to let our country live.

J says that the northern constellation Aquila, lying south of Cygnus, and containing the bright star Altair, appears in the formation of an eagle. Thus we are represented in the sky too.

Natural wonders frighten me: they are "unnatural wonders" for which I have no explanation. In school my teacher had said: ". . . the two agents that are responsible for Yellowstone National Park are fire and ice." I had imagined then that the mountains were actually huge ice sculptures, and the lakes formed from drippings melted off by the sun; I had pictured a ranging, transparent glassy park: hissing and splashing . . . simmering night and day.

I want to go to Emerald Pool, transparent purple-blue waters set in orange sand, to take color pictures. M will want to be in most of the pictures . . . he has his mother in mind when he poses.

"Gonna get me some of them obsidian arrowheads," M says.

I see M covered with obsidian arrowheads like porcupine quills; he is pit-patting on all fours through the school basement; he meets the custodian who is raising the thermostat as high as it can go; it is June, the sit-in at the school is still going on; the custodian wants to suffocate the students . . . to burn them with steam . . . make them run out into the street. He tells M to position himself just beyond the cafeteria doors, to shoot his obsidian arrowheads at the children as they try to flee. M agrees. However, the arrowheads are black soul-brothers

72

in another incarnation . . . they bury themselves in the wall to spell out the words: BLACK POWER!

M is trampled in the ensuing rush.

◉

"What if heavy snows sweep across the continental divide?" I ask M. "What if we go all the way there and find that the park entrances are closed?"

"Let me worry about that," he says. "I'll consult the Weather Bureau before we take off. There are wonders to be seen in the off-season too. I understand they use snowmobiles to get around."

◉

I am the deciduous quaking aspen. My fresh green trembling leaves have fallen off again and I am bare. My natural enemy is the beaver who eats me up inside, and then when I am hollow, floats me downstream to help build his dam. Squirrels nibble elegantly on my bark and buds. Mice embrace me, digging sharp claws in to maintain their balance. Birds eat my buds. Elk and deer also make a meal of me in times of famine. My once beautiful arms are left bare or scarred from forest fires or lightning.

I am Melissa Johnson: I am the deciduous quaking aspen.

◉

M's mother is not old. And she has more plants than the Botanical Gardens. She also has a cat called Smut. She is a slender woman in her late fifties, I think, but she passes for thirty something.

She is a widow.

She is ingenious.

Her home is filtered by an aura of palpable femininity.

When M was unemployable she supported us.

She is better than me in every way. I mistreat M to hurt her.

Her kitchen: Venetian blue and white tile.

Her living room: zebra rug, appliqued pillows, lattice-front armoire, live trees, potted plants, bamboo magazine rack, leopard ceramic doorstop, flower printed sofa in beige and green (that makes one feel one is "getting into a garden"), and her own paintings on the wall.

Her bedroom and dressing room: white bookcase containing a bright sweater collection, bracelets and beads on the wall, Porthault flowered sheets, old French chairs covered in lace and ruffles, and again, her own paintings on the walls.

Her studio: meticulously clean, color charts on the wall, an easel, a captain's chair, and a potted plant.

She owns a luxurious fur blanket on which she seduced M. It sheds.

In Yellowstone National Park, M assured the park ranger that he would not feed, touch, tease, or molest the black or the grizzly bear. And that he would not bury rubbish that smelled of food, for the bears to unearth. Yet, when I woke up suddenly where we had camped for the night, I found myself surrounded by the remains of our evening repast. A 900-pound grizzly was traveling toward me as if he had discovered his ideal gourmet meal: gopher stuffed with ants, mushrooms, berries, and mice.

I screamed just once before a shot rang out in the frigid air; M had killed the bear. The huge thing thrashed about in pain for a few minutes before it died. Amazing that grizzly cubs are born blind, naked, and helpless, weighing at the most one pound each.

"Why did you surround me with garbage? Did you want the bear to kill me?"

"No, my dear," M said, "I wanted to kill *it* with my new rifle, but I needed a decoy, and you did admirably well."

". . . and if you had missed?"

"I never miss!"

M packs the car the night before. His gun, sheer black-barreled ugliness, has the look of a killer. Its dull finish (nonreflective) is calculated not to betray the owner's presence. He snuggles the multishot, autoloading shotgun between two heavy woolen blankets. He wraps it with care: it has not always been well; when M first handled it, it coughed out five 12-gauge blasts till he put it down again. The baby spits bullets.

M drives to New Jersey to say good-bye to his mother. M lifts her in his arms. She squirms away.

"Not here. Not now," she says, leading the way to the

sofa. M sinks in: he is autumn: he is reds, golds, and browns in her garden . . . he is a fallen leaf about to be swept away by passion. She rakes him in.

If she keeps doing that, it will be all the reward he requires for staying alive. It has come to that.

◉

Follow the plantigrade spoor of M's fat feet and you will be able to read my story written in snow. M has gone for help. He has left me somewhere under a huge, wind-fluted snowdrift. It may seem that M is ambling aimlessly, but his purpose is to find a park ranger, and he does. They approach my lair from leeward. M scoops great chunks of compacted snow from the drift: brings a hatchet down with all his force to break through the ice-coated roof that has formed in his absence. I am dead.

To the surprise of the park ranger, M devours me immediately: his long canines crunch through my thin skull, till there is nothing left but two limp strands of hair and a pair of boots.

Abruptly the park ranger starts to chase M, who manages to cover a lot of ground in his peculiar, broad-legged, shuffling gait.

He climbs to the top of an iceberg.

He glissades down the other side, arms outstretched to break the descent. He is satiated and wants to sleep.

He advances toward a pressure ridge, careful to keep downwind and out of sight of the ranger. He lies for a moment on a large level stretch of ice. He inches forward.

Suddenly he freezes.

The ranger has spotted his big, shiny, red, pitted nose. The nose stands out.

"It is unmistakable miles away," the ranger says.

M hides it automatically. Without his nose he becomes another yellowish-white clump of snow fallen into human shape.

Inside of M, I get myself together.

The next morning both our flensed carcasses are found frozen into the ice.

Why won't M admit that we are a dying culture . . . he is completely out of touch with the fabric of America. The fabric he wraps himself in is all wool and a yard wide. Incredible. He is to be present at the hearing in which students advance their demands for a more meaningful educational program. I can imagine what that will be like!

At the hearing, the teachers and members of the board are seated on one side of the room. All are wearing jackets, even the dowdy ladies who make no attempt to hide their baroque-veined legs. They sit gingerly, as if protecting a distended, exquisitely tender protrusion. The students have been bearing down on them, and they expect no immediate relief. Their hair, in an expression of shock, rises short and stiff; their mouths gape open . . . fishlike. The jaws creak as words leak out of them: ". . . we cannot give in . . . ," "But we have agreed on . . . ," "The question is . . . ," "We are listening," "It is our belief," ". . . a deep-seated malaise!"

The students present their demands:

1. That the school employ more Third World instructors, e.g., gamblers, pimps, whores, chippies, madams, dining-car waiters, and Holy Rollers.

2. That there be a separate lunchroom serving Third World food, e.g., alligator tail & rice, chitterlings & collard greens and okra, barbecued ribs, pig's feet, chicken and drop dumplings with sweet potatoes, neckbones & lye hominy; desserts: sweet potato pie, watermelon, blackstrap sorghum molasses & biscuits; beverages: sassafras-root tea, homemade buttermilk.

3. That a zoo be built with city funds adjacent to the school in order that Third World students may become

acquainted with the vital, primitive force that stalks African jungles, e.g., lions.

4.　That there be taught a language of the Third World, e.g., Yoruba.

The members of the board agree that a gambler might be hired as a mathematics instructor. They quibble about whether the dining-car waiter would be sufficiently versed in geography to teach that subject, and they practically come to blows about using a pimp and a whore as social studies instructors. They are baffled and helpless. Chitterlings ding-a-ling past their awarenesses. Zoos harbor animals hungering to attack them. Yoruba speaks to them of coastal intrigue and bad black linguistic stock.

They turn down almost all of the demands.

M is taken hostage!

His head is forced through a hole that has been cut in a sheet. The sheet is hanging across a section of the gym.

Black Phys. Ed. students are taking potshots at M with a basketball. They wonder why he shows no dismay: does not try to withdraw or cry out. Why doesn't he?

He is dead.

He is nicer when he is dead. He is smiling and he has an erection. The sheet falls over him. He is ready for surgery. The barber sharpens his razor. M is emasculated. I shall hold two burials: one for his body, one for his sex. Because his sex is in such a tiny casket, I will have it interred in a pet cemetery.

⬤

It is obvious that nobody shall overcome nothing.

Violence for violence's sake. Well all right.

And you, Charles Thomas, though you're full of Third World demands, what the hell is a Third World? Just another cattle roundup.

⬤

M crawls around the house like a healthy cockroach: darting and stopping, darting and stopping. He has been eating away at my brain as if it were made of papier-mâché; as long as he and I are housed in the same apartment, he will not go hungry. He is perched on my head, all six legs clutching it as if it were a strawberry. He would not notice it if I reached up and squashed him.

"Explain these keys!" M demands. He has found them in my pocketbook. He had hoped to find something incriminating, and he has. I don't know whether I should tell the truth to Mr. Roach, or let him feel it out of me with his antennae. He would not even realize that truth is part of me . . . he would think it was a wall, a book, a shelf . . . his own truth, something for a roach to crawl over or eat the paint from.

Naturally I lie.

"These? These must be old keys. You know I never throw anything away. Probably from our apartment on East Broadway."

"We gave those to the new tenants," M says. He falls on his back as if poisoned. The couch groans with him. M has been frantic all day about another matter, the matter of his ouster from school. The students have gotten up a petition to remove him. So, he is focusing on me to relieve the tension. It doesn't do me any good.

M holds the keys up. They ring against each other. They are gold keys hung on an elastic ribbon. One has a round top, the other is oval with a knob above the hole. Both are serrated, lined, fluted, flattened, indented, duplicated, and named: Cole National.

Yes, I thought they would open the way to pleasure for me.

◉

Lita is so lovely. She has given me the keys to her apartment. She is a photographer and world traveler, I wonder why she is being so generous? Is she interested in me? She walks back and forth in the nude as she explains how to use the keys:

"Remember the gate downstairs, on the second floor? You can use the key, but you can also reach in and flip the latch with your fingers."

"Good," I say, "sounds easy."

She brings me a glass of Burgundy. It is pretty good American wine from California "11" Brands. It leaves no bitter taste. It leaves a hint of grape, which is probably what wine lovers mean by bouquet. It is elusive. Once I have decided that it is elusive, I drink it down like water, without tasting it at all. I don't want to pretend it is vintage, and must be savored. Wine bores me and puts me to sleep.

"This is where I keep the liquor. You're welcome to anything I have . . . whatever is in the refrigerator too."

Lita's kitchen is tiny. She cooks on a two-burner hot

plate. There is a small sink against the wall (she has to do her dishes immediately; there is no room for them to pile up in). A bunch of red onions hangs from a nail on the wall.

"And don't drink the milk; I think it's sour," she says. "Oh, and I've put clean towels in the bathroom . . . so just make yourself at home."

We go into the bedroom. She smiles knowingly at me, rips the bedspread off with a burst of energy. "I changed them for you," she says.

I imagine the tender sapling J, playing bridegroom; with me behind the softest of cambric veils. I thank the handmaiden Lita. She gives me additional information: the name of her hotel in Hawaii, in case her boyfriend calls and wants to know where she is; her maid's number; the number of her liquor store.

◑

Lita is gone, and I am in possession of the apartment. Yet I feel that she is watching me. That her sheets, her glasses, her telephone are receiving minute impressions of me for her. That after I leave, no matter how expertly her maid tidies the place, she will be able to smell my breath breathing back at her from the mouthpiece of the phone, taste my lips on her glassware, hold my body in her arms as if she is J.

●

My cousin writes to invite me to her home in Washington. M thinks I have accepted the invitation. Instead I go to Lita's apartment on 57th Street. J has promised to meet me there. It took me an hour on the phone to persuade him; he thinks he is seeing me for the last time. We've been through this before.

●

He is an hour late. Two wine glasses are set on the table. Music is playing. I am wearing a transparent blouse and no brassiere. I call J . . . June answers.

"How are you?" I ask, not ready to inquire about J . . . I am afraid that he has gone to a museum, or a movie, to avoid me.

"I have a foot infection," June says.

"How did that happen?" I ask, amazed that it is always the dancer's foot, or the pianist's finger, or the singer's throat that gets hurt or sick.

"I got mad at J for prowling around the house all day and not talking to me, and I kicked him. Tore a toenail . . . it got infected, that's what happened. Not very dramatic, but I had to cancel my class. I soak it every two hours. Say, could you hold the phone; I think I hear J at the door. I sent him shopping. Ah, good, here he is."

"Speak to you later then," I say, hanging up. So, it is not his fault he is late. I am happy all over again. I figure out how long it will take him to get to 57th Street. I give him half an hour.

Before the half hour is up, I go downstairs to wait between the two stores that are on either side of the house where Lita lives. It is a curious neighborhood to live in: nothing but places in which to spend large sums of money: banks, exclusive department stores such as Bendel's, art galleries, antique stores, import shops. To be honest, I must say that there is also, close by, a Chock full o' Nuts store. But this is a concession to the salesgirls and clerks who staff the expensive and chic places of business. I myself enjoy their shrimp-salad sandwiches, their chicken-salad sandwiches, and their tuna-fish-salad sandwiches, all of which taste exactly alike: like celery. I must look very suspicious, stepping in and out of the doorway, looking up and down the block to see if J is coming. My shoes are off and I'm juiced and I don't dare look too long in one direction, in case I miss him coming in the other.

I see him coming from the west. He must have taken the IRT and walked east.

"I thought you wouldn't be able to find it," I say.

"I found it," he answers.

When we go in I show him the gate trick. It clangs behind us. Then we walk up two additional flights.

I sit very close to him. He refuses a glass of wine. I kiss him. He draws away. I see he is going to be difficult.

"I thought you wanted to talk," he says coldly.

"I love you," I say. "I can't stand not touching you. All you have to do is come into a room and I know what it feels like to be had by a force of nature."

"You mean it?" His little-boy ego is flattered, even if he has come ostensibly to say good-bye; he wants his going to be pleasant, complimentary, an unnoticeable transition into "just good friends." He can't understand the attraction he has for me, or I for him. He thinks he can take one part of it, the sexual, and lock it away, leaving only our superficial conversations on science, astronomy, photography, mythology, politics to sustain us.

His smooth chest pleases me so much because M is so hairy.

I kiss his flesh even though he is being aloof. He is wearing his usual no undershirt, unbuttoned sport shirt outfit. I make him touch my breasts. They are so firm and young-looking. I want to go to bed with him in Lita's apartment . . . we would have all the time in the world . . . nobody to interrupt us.

"Jason," I say to him, "let me help you get your kingdom back."

"You know I hate to be called Jason," J says, pouting.

"C'mon, J, I'll help you get the golden fleece; don't you want it?"

J says, "No one can make the attempt and come back alive." J is playing games with me. He's okay now: he is not afraid of games. Only good boys are allowed to go out to play. J is a good boy. "How can you help me?"

I lead him into the bedroom. I am magical: I undress J and anoint his skin with so potent a salve that it will protect him from all harm; he will be able to retrieve the golden fleece.

He becomes excited.

He picks the fleece off a hanging branch with his sex, after I have sung a snake to sleep.

"If you are nice to me I will give you eternal youth," I say to J.

"How?" he asks, removing one sandal.

"I will always remember you exactly the way you are."

I do not want to remember J exactly as he is. But I promise.

I go down on him. He asks me to stop. He is very sensitive. His penis is wearing the golden fleece like a mantle. It has bugs in it. They are golden too. I pick them off one by one and cast them into a pillbox to save for threading a necklace. J gets bigger and bigger as I work around his sex. Finally his penis thrusts itself into my hand, as if it is the snout of an affectionate animal.

J turns traitor on me. He has an orgasm the minute he gets in.

"Didn't you notice I wasn't loving you?" he asks.

"No, I didn't notice it," I lie.

I have no rival: unlike Medea I have no one to send the lovely robe which envelopes its wearer in fearful devouring flames. I stand in front of J wearing that robe myself: I drop dead . . . my very flesh melted away.

"J," I say, ". . . you have an ugly body and an ugly mind. And all the time I was seeing you, I slept with M too."

He stares at me in disbelief. His naïveté had led him to believe that, because I loved him, I could not, and would not sleep with M. He took it for granted.

We dress quickly, and he offers to help me pack my bag. I tell him, "No, thank you." When I am done packing, he carries the bag downstairs for me.

As I step into my dragon-pulled chariot, I can see that he is full of anger. He has lost more than a friend and lover; he has lost a sorceress.

In one legend it is said that Jason committed suicide. But when did he begin to affect remorse?

Do you really mean NEVER, when you say never?

When I saw Lita yesterday, I said, "Lita, do you still have your old apartment?"

"My God, the building's been torn down," she answers.

Size forty-four men's boxer shorts in baby blue: M is furious.

"I don't wear a size forty-four!" he shouts.

"Let me measure you," I offer, but I do not have a tape measure, I have a piece of cord and a ruler. I make M stand so that I can circle his girth with my cord.

"I know my size," he says, sucking his belly in.

When I tell him that he measures $43\frac{1}{2}$ inches, he says, "You don't know how to measure. Why doesn't this house have any of the things other houses have . . . an ordinary tape measure?"

M lies down again. He asks me to measure him as he lolls there in fat. His belly flattens out. I measure forty-one inches. He is satisfied.

"Return those to the store tomorrow," M orders. "How did you ever imagine I was fat enough to wear the forty-fours?"

◉

I have by an extraordinary stratagem blown M up. As he balloons out, he makes a low hissing sound. His parts unfold and fill with air. I plug his asshole so it won't escape. He floats out the door. He is wearing, for propriety's sake, a size forty-four baby-blue pair of boxer shorts, out of which pops a shocking-pink latex erection. As he passes over 34th Street, children wave to him. He is then screened by a tall building, but reappears on the other side as an ill-defined obscurity: black smoke has laid its residue on him. I hear M pray for rain to wash his surface. He prays so hard his cork pops out.

He deflates.

He crumples to a rooftop, his skin rubbing together like the tissue of an empty stomach.

And a hole grows.

By the time I retrieve M, he is an empty pair of dirty underwear.

More underwear: this time it is J's T-shirt. He has forgotten it in my house. June made him wear it, so he lost it. The name tape pressed to the inside of the neckline says: CAMP GULLIVER. I actually blush when I read that. Last year he was young enough to go to camp. Oh, J! (J!)

J, I've decided to go to a football game with M. You're invited and so is Charles Thomas. Charles Thomas has shoulder pads and his own football to kick around. He blocks well. You're a natural fumbler. Want to play? You can fumble between the center and the quarterback. I've got a world of speed. M is on the offensive. He confuses me. I have trouble keeping out of his way. What I need is more grass drills and added weight.

J has just lost the ball again. How can he drop it? Charles Thomas has filled it with sand, that's how. He does not have to break J's arm. He does not have to take a crack at either elbow from underneath. But any method is valid if it makes the offense fumble. And J has lost the ball again. He doesn't get the point even though he has been trained to charge through a gauntlet of dozens of rubber straps that automatically whip at the football.

"I'd rather eat a hot dog in the stands," J says.

The sun beats down on our heads. M has taken off his shirt. His hair, gleaming in the sun, traps him behind miles of tangled burnished wire. He drinks beer. He drinks wine from a special picnic basket prepared at the Brasserie. Charles Thomas empties the basket, and puts it on his head to prevent sunstroke. He takes off his Dashiki. He is not wearing shoulder guards. He is balancing a sweet potato pie on each shoulder. He asks me to take a piece of pie without removing the pie plate from his shoulder. I cannot.

"Is it true that M killed you because you wouldn't sleep with him?" I ask Charles Thomas.

"I think it have more to do with three hundred black students learnin' to dance in the spotlight."

"Then why didn't he just kill the spot?"

"The spot don't bleed."

As I lie on the massage table, blue light from the sunroom spreads over the ceiling. I smell ultraviolet . . . alcohol . . . sweat . . . sesame seed oil. The masseuse zigzags one display of vitality after another, twisting handfuls of me, working the spine, hacking the fat with pseudo karate chops that leave me invigorated instead of relaxed.

Below each knee is an indented circle left there by the elasticized cuff of my knee socks. M bought them for me so that I might look like a schoolboy! They are part of an outfit which is very chic: a one-piece leather short overall.

"Turn over please," the masseuse says.

I have to tell myself that she's seen everything, before I lie on my back. M made me shave my pubic hair. I feel so naked.

"Had an operation?" the masseuse asks.

"Yes, but I have doctor's permission to take massage. You can be as rough as you like with me. Do everything you usually do."

Charles Thomas runs his tongue along the soles of my feet, between my toes: "I wouldn't do this if you wasn't clean," he says.

"I love it," I say. "I've loved it ever since I saw a handsome actor lick the stage. He loved the stage. He licked himself across the stage. I cried encore!"

Charles Thomas doesn't need applause. He hears those little patsy-watsy strokes dance off my skin, and takes a bow.

The masseuse assaults him as he bends down, as if she is supervising a toilet training session: she beats him about the buttocks, genitals, and head. However, he wets his pants for spite, and leaves an excremental offering in the tip plate. It is more than she usually receives.

"I wish people would stop fooling around with the air conditioning. God what conditions to work under!" the masseuse says.

J wheels the massage table down the corridor. He says I am running a fever and must be isolated. We are followed by Charles Thomas and the muscular masseuse. They each carry a bag of ice cubes to pack me in.

"Will you be here when I thaw out?" I ask J.

He melts the center of an ice cube with his hot young breath, and puts the cube on my finger. It sparkles.

"I'll always be here," he says, catching the ring drops as they weep from my finger.

The half-hour massage is over.

Yes, J, you have successfully isolated me.

J, darling.

If you play dead, you die.

Remember our first kiss?

I remember our first kiss in the Great Northern Hotel, on the steps that led nowhere. You ran up the stairs and knocked on the wooden panel, "Look," you said, "they don't go anywhere." It was your discovery . . . but, baby . . . things leading nowhere are prevalent . . . and people who are nowhere are boarded up behind useless stares . . . and old lovers are buried behind brick walls in abandoned cellars.

Forgive me.

M is drinking again. He began at the football game. I have to be careful; he is armed and dangerous. We are locked into the apartment. If he begins sniping out the window . . . M says that he doesn't care whether he lives or dies. I care. I don't want to see him punched full of holes as he tries to run for cover.

Once we traveled across the country, and in most small diners or groceries where we stopped, they sold chances: a punchboard stuffed with tiny rolled-up names.

The idea was to punch out a winning name. We punched Winnie; the winning name turned out to be Blanche. The waitress lifted a small round seal at the top of the punch-board to prove to us that the winning name really was Blanche.

No matter how many holes are punched in M, he can't win. But he can lose with more chances than anyone.

"Let me call your mother?" I plead. M pulls the telephone wire out of the wall. There goes his last chance. She could have lured him out of the house with the promise of a warm bath and a back rub . . . and a cartridge belt still warm from being strapped across her naked hips. That's where she stores her lipsticks, each one an amorous bullet of color loaded with kisses meant to explode in M's face. I used to wonder what caused the gap below his nose. It isn't an ordinary mouth; it hasn't healed: there are teeth missing, and his gums bleed.

"Where's the champagne?" M asks. I bring a bottle of New York State champagne that was stashed away for our anniversary. May as well celebrate death. . . death is the long-awaited occasion. I pop the cork for M.

M has a bilateral temporal EEG abnormality. He experiences the sound of a ringing bell as a seizure aura. Occasionally he hears the same bell when he feels like exhibiting his penis. A doctor told me that compulsive genital display is linked to abnormal discharges in the temporal area. It was suggested that he be lobotomized. I did not agree that the punishment fitted the crime.

I reread the letter Charles Thomas has sent me from South Africa. I have locked myself in the toilet. When I am done with the letter, I will tear it up and flush it away. If M suspects that I am a friend of Charles's he will kill me.

Dear Miss Melissa Johnson,

I'm lucky I'm alive. I was number 2001 to line up for going down the diamond mine. 50 men in front of me stumbled and fell over one another. Most got crushed. The narrow tunnel they died in leads directly from where we sleep in barracks to the mine.

I want you to tell my friends in the USA to picket the Chimerical Bunk New York Trussed Company

for their support of South Africa's apartheid establishment. . . . Chimerical Bunk also joined with
Chaste Manhattan and Thirst National Titty to lend
$40 million directly to the South African Govern-
ment.

Make a big sign, sugar . . . carry it for me.

No chance of copping a diamond down here:
these cats investigate everybody's shit with a fine-
toothed comb. Later, baby.

Charles

There is guilt by association. I remember Lew Harris's
wife asking me to empty my handbag on her table. She
wanted to make sure I wasn't packing a pistol. Wish I
had one now. What would I do with it? Shoot myself out
of the toilet?

The bullet might shatter an object of great sentimental
value. A gift J gave me. He made it himself . . . a clay
sculpture of a cat. The cat is curled up (J's favorite
position). June and I marveled at how well done it was. I
told M I bought it in the Village.

J has found a way to capture the sun's rays and separate them. He has made a chromo lens. The lens is made of glass which is double convex and hollow; it is seven inches in diameter and will hold forty-two ounces. He has made it in different colors, but, he says, "It does not constitute a lens until filled to the neck with a transparent liquid." When hanging in the sun, it receives the most exquisite medical elements into the water according to its color. It is potent. J is a scientific genius; he has also built a color wheel with removable discs (every color of the spectrum). He says that for every color there is a corresponding drug, for example:

Red, arterial stimulant—drug, ammonia.
Orange, lung builder—drug, carbonate of lime.
Yellow, cathartic—drug, calomel.
Yellow-green, cleanser—drug, chlorides.
Blue-green, cleanser—drug, boric acid.
Blue, alleviator of pain—drug, citric acid.
Indigo, astringent—drug, aconitum.
Violet, motor nerve depressant—drug, opium.
Yellow-violet, digestant—drug, chloral hydrate.
Violet-red, emotional stabilizer—drug, digitalis (foxglove).
Blue-red, cardiac energizer—drug, potassium nitrate.

I do not believe his claim that blue-charged water can cure an obstinate case of dandruff! June places J directly in front of the blue disc to quiet his nerves.

J says, "Blue vibrates 658,000,000,000,000 (trillion) times per second."

June says, "Although the green rays are good for head colds, boils, croup, eyestrain, hay fever, whooping cough, and nerve exhaustion, it aggravates cases of insanity."

She is staring fixedly at my green dress. This is a humane reason for me to remove my clothes. I don't know what to do about my mouth which I have rinsed with a chlorophyll mouthwash. June gives me a glass of solarized milk to neutralize my breath. I give off a philosophical yellow aura. J is calmed by my presence.

There is a red disc on the color wheel. My love and I bask in its sexy hot rays.

J is jealous of Charles Thomas. He knows I am seeing him. It prompts him to discuss the color black. "What kind of world would we be living in if it were composed of black, brown, and gray? Black clouds fill me with terror. Black means concealment and repression: the negation of pure spirit. It indicates hatred, malice, revenge, and low feelings . . . 'dark forces' . . . 'black magic' . . . necromancers (those who deal out death) . . . black is foreign and hostile to life."

J is a poor example of the infinite power of life and love. He has lost his center of luminosity.

J is at June's dance concert. There is no stage. It is in a loft. We are seated on the floor. There are two ladders among us. The concert has not yet begun. J is seated next to me against the wall. We are hugging our knees. J stands up. He takes a young girl by the hand, pulls her toward me as if she is a toy on wheels. I expect her to make a quacking sound every time the wheels go round. J hands me the string. I tentatively jerk her toward me. J has brought me an educational toy, one I would like to take apart and not put together again.

"This is Noreen," he says, introducing her to me.

They stand there adoring each other . . . pressing hands the way J and I used to. Is he innocent? Or is he trying to hurt me? Or are they part of the dance concert?

The lights go out.

From my seated position I kiss J's knees, his thighs; I put my hand up his trouser leg; he limps away as if I am an old war injury. The fourteen-year-old girl and J merge, wearing the same shadow. . . .

June and three men, all in white overalls, enter: they cross each other's paths diametrically. June drags one ladder to another spot; she walks under it. The remaining ladder is rushed by the three male dancers . . . they knock it down and climb on it as it lies collapsed upon the floor.

The lights go out.

A flood spot goes on.

June is seen on the top rung of a ladder. She takes a paper flag out of her overall pocket and waves it. She has conquered a mountain, a moon, a parade . . . the men bear her away on the ladder.

We drink weak punch and ask, "Did you like it?"

I ask J, "Did you like it?"

With a question like that there is always a divergence of opinion. The young girl answers, "Like what?"

⬤

J leaves with the girl. We are to remain apart for a while. June approves of the separation . . . my affair with J is incestuous.

⬤

When we were first married, we had no furniture, but we had a sense of order, so we bought two large cardboard cartons: Singlewall F74. We marked one SUMMER, and the other WINTER. Into the WINTER carton we put the heavy things. I am lighter than M, so when he was angry with me, he'd bury me in the SUMMER carton with my belongings. At first this frightened me:

I'd be afraid of smothering. After a year of being packed away, I used to race for SUMMER whenever M's eyebrows joined in a furry peak above his nose. I got to love being in the box: being in the box was not like being anywhere else.

Was not like being.

A woman.

A box.

I resist the idea of buying a vibrator, though orgasmic one-upmanship intrigues me. I want to break my record. There are two kinds of vibrator that I know of: the one that looks like a blind flashlight, and the one that has a water-cooled motor (and rides strapped to your hand). The latter palsies the hand itself, so that when masturbating, you can vibrate your genitals into orgasm without tiring. The other makes its dull presence known by filling the space and jarring it!

I imagine spending long sultry afternoons alone with my mechanical Robot . . . eventually, after long intimacy, daring to call it Rob.

M comes home early one sultry afternoon, and follows the plugged-in electric cord to the bed, where I am busy reaching plateau after plateau of joy.

"Bitch . . . butch . . . borscht . . . botch!"   he insults my body.

"Don't you dare talk that way to me!" I shout indignantly. "Can't you see that I'm well connected?"

There are two bowls on the table. One is turned over. The inverted bowl has captured the demons that torment J. The empty bowl is a writ banishing me from my marriage to M. Written on the bowl is the statement that I am forthwith expelled stark naked and with disheveled hair.

So that I can do no more harm, M hires an artist to draw a picture of me on the bowl, nude, with flying hair, my arms tied, and feet chained.

We have corn flakes for breakfast in ancient crockery.

"You want to be better than I am," M accuses, as I manage to open a jar of pickles he has failed with. I should have heeded *Cosmopolitan*'s warning to women: NEVER OPEN A JAR YOURSELF IF THERE IS A MAN HANDY. APPEAR HELPLESS, HE LIKES IT THAT WAY.

Because of the jar of pickles which I so rashly attacked and conquered, I suppose that M is not going to date me again. He was about to take me to see *The Wild Bunch* (advertised as a "blood ballet").

"I don't want to be you at all," I say. His remark is a commonplace . . . a masculine idea . . . I am already better than he is.

I have never wanted to own a penis: out of curiosity I hold a banana out front to see what it would be like. It looks strange . . . it is in danger of being lopped off, or at least peeled. I think it will last longer if it is not peeled (peeled it will grow rotten faster, or somebody will eat it up). In all fairness to penises, breasts also are in danger of being lopped off. People who stand out are in danger

106

too: I don't have to name those who were cut down in their prime.

◍

Prima-vera.
Must we all be the same in order to exist together?
Prima-inter-pares.
I am first among equals.

◍

M says that God did not create woman from man's rib, since the rib is still there.

◍

I am the marrow and the splint. I am everybone. I am the tissue and the lie. I am everybone. I am the cartilage and the cap. I adapt to bear the strain of pressure. I glide smoothly. I provide support. I am the skeleton. I am everybone. I am twelve pairs of ribs. I let man breathe. I afford strength: the humerus. I afford strength: the femur. My pelvis is a basin. I wash the human race.

I am:

skull

cervical vertebrae

clavicle

scapula

sternum

ribs

humerus

ulna

radius

ilium

sacrum

coccyx

pubis

ischial tuberosity

femur

patella

tibia

fibula

calcaneus:

I am the skeleton in God's closet.

I am also woman who is interested in structures: in the architecture of survival. And I know that M wants to disown me. He would be happiest in an all-male world.

"You're soft and boneless," M says to me.

"I'll rattle same as you when I'm dead," I say.

M pinches me to show how soft I am. I cook supper.

⬤

Sometimes Charles Thomas's patina varies from red to black, sometimes mat, sometimes shiny (when he makes love he is polished). His esteemed color is not merely ornamental; it gives a clue as to his life: he has been used.

⬤

"I once had a real mother when I was twelve years old," Charles says to me. "She was a great lady."

"I didn't know you knew your real mother," I say.

"Didn't you know I was with her till I was thirteen?" He takes my hand and looks sincerely into my eyes. I interpret the look as being a sincere one.

"My husband told me that you just found out that you are a foster child."

"He's lyin' in his teeth," Charles Thomas says.

"Oh, I'm so glad," I say, and kiss the tip of his ear.

"I can prove it," he says. "You know how great my

mom was? Remember, she is a black woman, with none a those white hang-ups; well, I was a pretty naïve twelve-year-old, and I was in my room, by myself, masturbating. I never done it before. I didn't know what it was . . . I came out of the room with this white stuff in my hand, and I showed it to my mom. 'Mom, what's this stuff?" I asked her. 'That's your seed, son,' she said. 'That's life comin' out.' I love my mother. I got no complaints."

◉

Charles Thomas takes me to the cemetery where his mother is buried. He can't find her grave. "Guess she don't have no tombstone," he says.

We stand above an unmarked grave that may be hers. I have brought an offering; it is a Karner butterfly mounted behind glass: brown, edged in white, with brushings of blue on the wings; there are ten sections of blue on its double round tail, ending in tiny cuticles of red above brown dotted tips. J netted it as it was resting on a heavenly blue lupine, in full bloom, on the valley floor of Yellowstone National Park.

"What was your mother like?" I ask.

"Not like this," he says, as he lays the Karner butterfly to rest on a dry mound of earth. "She were more like a owlet moth: dark and grimy from the places she live in. In a few hundred years, if the air don't get no cleaner, all you Ofays gonna be black. It's a fact."

⬤

J has decided to go to the moon. It is the refuge, the true homeland of lunatics.

"But what will you do up there?" I imagine that he will bounce over the lunar landscape like silly-putty.

"Oh, I'll bounce around, take a dip in the Sea of Tranquillity. And I'll be laden with hand tools, camera, and antennae, including an Early Apollo Scientific Experiments Package, which will transmit information to earth. It's something I've always wanted to do."

He models his own special lunar surface suit with its associated "portable life-support system."

"You'll be lonely," I say, peering into his helmet.

"No, I won't! I'm not the only one going; they're sending the Chronics, the Incontinents, the Orphaned-Others, the Addictesses, the Inconsolables, and the Indigents, on sister flights. We're the new pioneers. Once they didn't know what to do with us . . . there was no room on earth . . . now we are to take our place in history, when there is unlimited space."

"So, you are going to leave me!"

"With great speed: three thousand, one hundred mph, as I round the eastern rim of the moon. But we'll keep in touch . . . my multiple electronic-umbilical system will maintain the link between us . . . between us . . . between us . . . between us. . . ."

⊕

M and I are in bed. As soon as he gets an erection, I slip out of bed. He joins me. We stand face to face.

"Why did you get out of bed? Why?" he asks.

I take hold of his erection and crank it up and down.

"The prick lifts the man," I say, laughing. "It's the leverage theory."

M illustrates my theory. He stretches taller and taller.

⊕

M's breath is being conveyed in sealed tanks from Washington to upper New York State. Dissident groups object, saying that in case of an accident (the tanks are going by rail) whole townships may be endangered. I know that M's breath is bad, but I hadn't suspected it was lethal.

M denies it is his breath they have managed to derail.

"What is it then?" I ask, pointing to the bill of lading.

"Farts from the last world war," M answers.

◍

"No, I can't sleep," I tell M.

"I'll stay up with you," M says.

The phone rings. It is Lita. Unusual for her to call so late. "I'm ill," she says. "I must have some warm milk and there are no grocery stores open in my neighborhood. Could you possibly bring me a quart of milk?"

I have an extra quart of milk. I put it in a bag.

"Where do you think you're going?" M asks, putting himself between me and the door. I explain about Lita, making her sound far sicker than she is. I want to get out! M lets me go after I promise to bring back the morning papers.

Lita is not alone. She is with a man. She feels fine.

"What am I supposed to do with the milk?" I ask. It is warming in my arms. Lita kisses me on the lips and takes the milk container away. Her friend kisses me on the lips too. Sitting between them on the antique couch, I begin to feel erotic and examine the living-room chandelier around which Lita has twisted flowers.

"Would you like something to drink?" Lita asks me.

"No."

"Some herb tea?"

"No."

The man stands up.

"Why don't we go to the bedroom; it's more comfortable in there," Lita says. She takes my arm and whispers into my ear, "Be nice, you'll have a good time. Paul is a lovely person . . . he loves to make love."

I've always wondered whether Lita's photography supported her entirely. As I watch Paul precede us, familiarly, to the bedroom, I surmise that he is a semi-customer.

To get to the bedroom we go through a narrow hallway which is also the bathroom, containing a bath-shower on the left, and a beveled glass window on the right. The toilet is small and separate. I excuse myself and go into the toilet. Lita has decorated it with life studies of nudes, and pornography. I wash my hands, and as they soap each other I THIMK sex.

"I'm going to take my clothes off," Lita says, doing so immediately. "Would you like to take your clothes off?"

"No," I say.

"What's the matter with you tonight?" Lita asks. "You didn't want anything to drink, and now you won't take your clothes off." She laughs at me, and brazenly shows herself off. She stands in front of the huge four-poster brass bed, cupping both breasts in her hands. "Paul, make her take her clothes off!"

Paul embraces me. He draws my hand over his erection. "It's for you," he says, "if you take your clothes off."

Dumbly I refuse. I am not comfortable with strangers.

He undresses. They tussle on the bed, giggling and whispering. They grab me. I fight back. They can't believe it. Neither can I.

"Don't be a drag," Lita says. "We won't hurt you. We just want to play . . . like little children."

The Tiffany lamp is softly glowing. The large mirror swinging between heavy mahogany posts is waiting for my naked image.

"Put out the light," I say . . . my one condition.

"Your friend is definitely lower class," Paul says to Lita as he turns off the light.

He lies beside me.

Where is Lita?

She is kissing me.

He puts his penis in.

Where is Lita?

She is kissing his ass.

He likes it. It makes him more excited. But he is concentrating on me, and ignoring her. She falls to the floor.

"You have a beautiful cunt," he says to me.

"Is he clean?" I ask Lita.

"He's a friend of mine," she answers.

"Where are my pants?" I ask frantically. It is late and I have to get back to M. We look on all the chairs, in the bed, on the floor. The pants cannot be found.

"Oh, I know," Lita says. She pulls them out from under the bed. "The dog likes to chew on panties."

I put them on even though they are wet from dog spittle. Semen drips from me, making them even wetter. I plan to toss them into the wash as soon as I get home . . . to sleep with M immediately . . . that way, if I get pregnant, M will think the child is his.

There is a tendency to think of strangers as someone you don't know. Yet, Charles Thomas and M know each other; but what do they know? M has not understood me for some time. He thinks my momentary moods: elation, depression, occur because I am reacting to him. I am not. I am reacting to my own chemistry. I would like to confide the vicissitudes of my life to him, but he might succumb to hating me and my friends, because of a little anecdote like this one, for instance . . . a trifle that is only mildly amusing; Lita and I are in a restaurant where they know her. She has invited me to be her guest. We are served our drinks fast enough, but after that, somehow the waiter ignores us. "I'll get his attention." Lita says. She takes off her blouse, under which she is wearing a see-through plastic bra. "It's the top of a bathing suit." She explains. "It sticks to me, but it looks great, doesn't it?" I touch it. The waiter comes over. "We'd like to give our orders now," Lita says. We order melon and hearts of artichoke with lemon, and no main course. Lita rebuttons her blouse. "You know," she says disgustedly, "once I was the only one who'd flash tits in public, now everyone's doing it, and they consider me the Establishment."

The school auditorium: students are about to watch experimental films made by their peers. Each will have a specific theme: Communication, Freedom, Love, Peace, and Happiness.

Charles Thomas is working the projector; he has also contributed a can of film. His theme is Love. And the title of his movie is: *The Holy Triad*. It runs twenty-two minutes, is in black & white, 16mm.

M is seated in the darkened auditorium. He is one of the instructors planted there to keep order if things get out of hand. He is clutching his briefcase, which contains test papers, official forms, textbooks, and a hand gun (nestling in a leather side pocket).

The auditorium smells like a gymnasium. M is used to that. He takes a deep breath and gets comfortable. *The Holy Triad* is the first film on the program. M imagines it is about the father, the son, and the holy ghost played by blacks. He thinks this derisively and feels superior. The movie begins:

THE HOLY TRIAD

Shadowy figures enter a temple. It is surmounted with long golden tubes resembling the pipes of an organ or a brass bed. There is an investiture in reverse going on: the removal of trappings, and the retention of holy apparel which fits like skin. Because of a softly glowing lamp, fringed decently to conceal its bulbs, the religious personages are seen for a time only as black silhouettes. One of the personages falls to his knees, praying or imploring his prelate at extremely close range: their bodies are as

118

one. The third divine is adhering to a strict routine of asepsis by drinking a murky purgative from his chalice.

M wishes the film were sharper visually. He formulates post-projection questions to ask the students in the audience. He wonders whether the film is saying something that he misses. He makes a few notes on a scrap of paper in the semidarkness of the auditorium, then continues to watch.

The purged cleric whispers a supplication into the ear of the kneeling prelate. He rises. All prostrate themselves before the temple of the Holy See . . . roll in a religious agony upon an imbricate velvet rug (its overlapping parts shot through with gold). A dog . . .

Symbolic of what? M tries to recall what he knows about Luis Bunuel and his use of the dog as a symbol.

. . . appears from under the dais with a holy relic in its teeth. The fragment, obviously the surviving memorial of a sacred person, is snatched from the dog's mouth and returned to its reliquary, where it may be preserved as worthy of veneration.

As the movie ends, a chorus of hallelujahs swells to fill the auditorium. M mounts the steps leading to the stage, grasps a lectern at each side, leans forward, and begins to pose the questions he has jotted down on the scrap of paper:

What does the triangle mean to you?

Is this a religious film?

What did the symbols you noticed point to?

Do you think that this film is a good visual prayer?

Does it express anything about communication between God and man?

But, Charles Thomas has made an experimental film, and the end is only the beginning. Even as M recites his penetrating questions, the film, frame by frame plays across M's broad, shiny forehead . . . this time everything is in sharp focus. M leaves the stage, returns to his seat, and faces the screen.

He does not see a religious allegory.

He does not see the triangle as a tendency of the universe to converge toward a point of unity.

He sees me, my best friend Lita, and a bare-assed male fucking each other on a big brass bed!

The dog has stolen my panties.

A superwave of shame hits M, yet he watches in shocked fascination as the film reveals to him what he has already imagined more than once. Rage fills him. He shoves his way through the whistling, sucking, banging, shouting students who are having a ball. Charles Thomas has made a grand coup!

M rushes upstairs to the projection room. The door is locked. He pounds on it with all his might as the film continues.

"You ever been blackmailed by a black male?" Charles Thomas asks.

"Are you referring to that shitty little sexploitation movie you made at Lita's?" I ask.

"Yeah."

"What kind of a price tag do you put on it?"

"At least a three-million-dollar bill!"

"Are you asking for that kind of financing on the basis of 'name' performers?"

"Yeah!"

M's mother is painting a portrait of him from memory and photographs. The photographs are pinned to her bulletin board, and spread on the floor. She works with fast intense strokes; she attacks the canvas. M's face appears to be that of a cherub: pink and smooth.

"He doesn't look that way anymore," I say.

"What do you know about it?" she retorts, adding a dot of white to his eye so that it sparkles. She is concerned only with saving him in art.

"The cops searched our apartment and found a pistol," I say. She shakes her head in good-humored disbelief.

The portrait progresses. What began in natural light is flooded with artificial.

"He's an excellent subject," his mother says. "He can hold a pose for hours." There is no wind to ruffle the photographs. Her breath, as she scrutinizes the photographs, causes them to flutter and shift. She returns to the canvas: the photographs settle. He has always obeyed her covert instructions.

From a long way off, over days, months, years, he comes hastening toward her, "There, now I have him. Don't you think it's him?" She steps back, measuring proportions with a paintbrush, holds it in front of her. She then gazes through a refraction glass . . . he retreats.

"Yes," she says. "Yes."

J says: "You must free yourself from the tomb of the flesh before you can range the cosmos at will . . . like me."

I say: "But I have not yet admitted that I have a body."

122

J must tour the zodiac alone. Sirius, the Dog Star, lights the way, but eats five pounds of meat daily, and bites strangers. Sirius is a swift and high-nosed dog of great beauty. J has sent me from the heavenly workshop a carving of Sirius in pigstone, a limelike substance mixed with sulfur which, when rubbed, gives off a smell of cat urine, rotten eggs, and sulfur. I place the carving next to my copy of *A Diary from Dixie*. I open it to page 213 by chance. I say to myself, "Whatever I read will be oracular and eternal." Then I read the line: "Battle after battle results in disaster after disaster. Every morning's paper reports enough to kill a well woman, or to age a strong and hearty one." True.

The monsoon rains have started like a rain of bullets. The wind blows from the southwest on M, in his Laotian garrison. He has gone where it is not only legal to kill, but mandatory. And he has escaped the police for a while. But the monsoon rains have started, and it is particularly disconcerting to fight in the midst of devastation to create more devastation. M likes it.

M likes to see whole trees in motion, almost breaking.

As the air fills with spray and the sea is covered with streaking foam, M loads his gun.

At home, I keep busy making batik . . . I hand-print cotton cloth painstakingly with hot wax and dye. I have been at it for six months. Charles Thomas has been taunting me: he calls, and when I say that I don't want to see him, he serenades me with "Yankee Doodle," accompanying himself on a bamboo instrument called an Aklung. His version of "Yankee Doodle" plays havoc with the old political verse:

> Yankee Doodle went to war
> Stuffed with hot baloney
> He stuck a finger up his ass
> And pulled out lots of money.

M's garrison has been captured by the Pathet Lao and North Vietnamese . . . it is a landmark in the war for the Communists. Now, I hear, there will be no letup; the Communist troops will be able during the October–April dry season to recapture the territory they held before the 1962 Geneva agreement—the northern two-thirds of the country. I am a war widow.

June once said to me: "If you didn't want to be with M, you wouldn't be. You are not forced to stay with him."

Of course she's wrong.

"J, you wait outside."

It is J's birthday. I go into the French bakery to pick up a cake I ordered for him; it has real butter-cream icing, and is decorated with a moon scene: two plastic astronauts beside a rocket. It is a little boy's cake. The vanilla icing (titanium and pearl) resembles the surface of the moon. The French, using only pure ingredients, have baked a fresh planet; we shall be the first to taste it. (Which proves you can destroy your planet and share it too.)

"Where shall we eat it?" I ask J. He wonders where the best place would be, then says, "Let's go back."

"Back where?" I ask.

"Follow me," he says.

I follow J back many eons. "If we go too far back, the cake will spoil," I say.

"We'll eat it as we go," J declares.

FIRST BITE:	J is in the water; he is no different than the swollen crumbs floating around him. He is evolving. He is in my womb. It will take him nine months to crawl out. Before his lungs inflate, his gills will heal shut and his element will no longer be water, but air and earth.
SECOND BITE:	J is in the water, but he cannot drown: I am growing him to save him. Twice, I have given birth to him, and twice kept a piece of the umbilical cord. Before it was tied and cut, I painted it gentian violet. Now, in my hand it has turned to leather.
	"Is that really what tied me to you?" J asks, lacing his shoes with it.
	"Don't be irreverent," I caution him.
THIRD BITE:	J is no longer the size of an English pea. It is the eighth week, in which he has become a fetus. Before this time it would have been impossible to determine by observation whether he was going to be a human being, a pig, a goat,

a dog, or a monkey. See how undetermined he really was before I took him into me.

FOURTH BITE: He looks very funny . . . all slits . . . bulging high forehead . . . asexual. A calcifying shrimp out of the shell.

FIFTH BITE: J is a parasite: he accepts my maternal contributions: food, shelter, a sewage system.

SIXTH BITE: He floats within the closed membrane which absorbs shock, and rearranges his position. His ear becomes functionally alive: it allows him to balance himself. How did he become unbalanced? "I cut off my ear and gave it to you," J says.
"Don't be irreverent about equilibrium," I caution.

SEVENTH BITE: I am constantly aware of J's movements. I have been spying on him for three months. "Why were you having me followed?" J asks.
"I wanted to deposit a layer of fat beneath your lean skin, so that you'd survive in the external world. You had lost

EIGHTH BITE: your covering of silky hair." J weighs five pounds. His nails project: they are soft and bendable. His body is rounded, his skin is no longer red . . . but he is not complete. He is correlated in the tenth and last lunar month before his birthday; it is then that the finishing touches are accomplished.

NINTH BITE: J comes out. It is a boy . . . it is a triumph of Y over X. "Did I hurt you?" J asks, offering me the last bit of birthday cake.

"Yes," I answer. "During the second stage."

J throws the plastic moon scene away. "I'm no longer a child!" he insists spitefully.

"Well then, kiss me and prove it," I say.

Before M comes home, I sweep away the crumbs and vacuum the couch. I look in the mirror. My face is red. I'm still excited. J and I had intercourse in the seated position. He gets more sophisticated every day.

M is holding on to his job. They won't allow him to teach, but they have assigned him to lunchroom duty. He is the supervisor, and is expected to create a smooth-functioning lunchroom.

The new lunchroom is in the basement. All windows are screened from the inside. There are two entrance-exits. Five hundred students fill the lunchroom each lunchroom period. This leaves little room for unrestricted movement by the students. All doors leading to the food area are shut about ten minutes prior to the ringing of the warning bell. Students are directed over a loudspeaker when to line up for food. Silverware tokens must be purchased for twenty-five cents at the beginning of the term. The silverware token is exchanged for a set of silverware by the cashiers at the time food is purchased. Three or four calls for silverware are made at intervals over the loudspeaker system, at which time the students are to return the silverware to a specified area and given their tokens in return.

The lunchroom has been divided into six sections. Walls adjacent to the tables are marked with a large letter: A, B, C, D, E, or F. The seniors sit in section A. This remains constant. Each student must register for a permanent seat at a table in his designated section. Any student failing to register is subject to disciplinary action.

This is the perfect job for M.

Dear Mrs. Johnson,

I expect you to meet me at Times Square for a silent vigil at 7 P.M. today. We'll walk with candles up Sixth Avenue to the Central Park lake at 60th Street and Fifth Avenue, where the Lantern Boat Ceremony will begin at 9 P.M.

You are invited to construct your own lantern boat beforehand if you wish. Instructions are: paper sides top and bottom, board at bottom 4" across (with candles stuck on; height of sides 7"). Peace messages and designs around outside of lanterns requested.

Enclosed, please find flier explaining the Lantern Boat Ceremony.

Sincerely,
Mr. Charles Thomas

Peace Message for a Lantern

WELCOME   WELCOME   WELCOME
   ALL   ALL   ALL

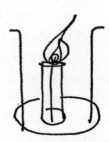

The Lantern Boat Ceremony is a reenactment of the Japanese Bon Festival, a traditional Buddhist observance. The festival has its origins in ancient India where it was celebrated at the end of the monsoon season and marked a time of reflection and rededication upon the resumption of normal daily pursuits. In Japan it has become a festival for honoring one's dead ancestors, praying for peace, and celebrating the spirit of giving. Since the war, in Hiroshima and Nagasaki the Bon Festival has become the annual commemoration of those who died in the nuclear disasters of 1945. Relatives of those who were lost float lanterns on the rivers of the cities in memory of their loved ones and as a prayer for world peace.

Charles Thomas and I meet secretly at the water's edge. We put our lanterns in the water. They float out to join other lanterns bobbing like giant fireflies in the lake.

"I don't have no dead ancestors," Charles Thomas says. "They all alive and well in Mississippi. My grandma is one hundred and six years old, my grandpa is one hundred and twenty, and I ate one hundred and sixty-nine pancakes with melted butter on them."

"What does a full stomach have to do with a full life?" I ask Charles Thomas.

"Well, let me explain," he says. "Let's go sit on the grass."

We sit on a hill not far from the lake, where we can still see the lanterns. Charles Thomas sits with his back comfortably against a tree. I lie down, my head in his lap. He speaks in a gentle lulling voice, as if recounting a bedtime story to a beloved child.

Once upon a time there was a black boy in Harlem, where black children abound, and hunger is an everyday affair. This little black boy had a black mother. And his black mother got him a beautiful little used red coat donated by the welfare, and a beautiful little pair of torn jeans, and a beautiful cracked plate to eat off of, and a lovely little pair of sturdy charity shoes with rubber soles and no linings. And then wasn't Little Black Charles grand! But he was hungry. So he put on all his fine clothes and went out for a walk in the jungle to see what he could cop. And by and by he met a pusher who said to him, "Little Black Charles, you wanna be really grand?"

"Sure do," Little Black Charles said.

"You wanna get you some lovely little purple shoes with crimson soles and paisley linings?"

"Sure do," Little Black Charles said.

"You wanna get you some groovy threads that the other cats gonna throw up with envy when they dig you comin' down the street?"

"Sure do," Little Black Charles said. "Whut I gotta do to get all that stuff?"

"All you gotta do is make some deliveries for me . . . but you gotta be circumspect . . . dig?"

"I'm hip!" Little Black Charles said.

"You gonna make your mamma a happy lady," the pusher said. He gave the little boy a package, and an address, and sent him on his way. But somewhere along Lenox Avenue, Little Black Charles met a big Honky-Nark.

"Where you goin', Little Black, an' what you got in that package?" the Honky-Nark asked.

"I ain't goin' nowheres, and I ain't got nothin' in that package," Little Black Charles answered.

And the Honky-Nark said to him, "Little Black, I'm goin' to eat you up, even though you're dark meat and probably on the tough side, unless you give me that package."

And Little Black Charles said, "Oh! Please, Mr. Honky-Nark, don't eat me up, and I'll give you my beautiful little red coat with three buttons down the front and a pocket for each hand. You kin have it for your own kin . . . only don't do me no harm."

"I ain't got no use for that stinkin' rag," the Honky-Nark said. "Give me that bag you're holdin' so tight."

So Little Black Charles he run as fast as his little legs could carry him, away from the growlin' Honky-Nark who was takin' perfect aim at his head with a revolver. But Little Black Charles run so fast he whizzed up the street faster than the speed of bullets. He ran away, sayin', "It sure hard to get to be the grandest Little Black in the jungle."

And Little Black Charles went on, and by and by he met another Honky-Nark, and his heart beat faster with fear because he was afraid this Honky-Nark would burn him, and then his beautiful black mamma would never get to be a happy lady.

"Little Black, I'm gonna eat you up, even though you're dark meat, and dark meat don't agree with me, unless you give me that package you're holdin'," the Honky-Nark said.

And Little Black Charles said, "Oh! Please, Mr. Honky-Nark, don't eat me up, and I'll give you my beautiful little pair of torn Wrangler jeans for your very own."

"I ain't got no use for those trousers, unless I give them to a more deservin' little black boy. Here, come closer and let me examine them." But Little Black Charles knew the Honky-Nark was tryin' to hype him, so he took off down the street as fast as his little legs could carry him. He ran away, sayin', "I gettin' to be the speediest Little Black in the jungle, but when do I get to be the grandest Little Black in the jungle?"

And Little Black Charles went on, and by and by he met another Honky-Nark, and it said to him, "Little Black Charles, I'm goin' to smear the sidewalk with you unless you give me that suspicious package whut you holdin' under your arm." And Little Black Charles made a sound like a baby burpin' and said, "Oh! Please, Mr. Honky-Nark, don't smear the sidewalk with me, and I'll give you my prized possession, this recently repaired, sturdy pair of lace-up oxfords. They make a thoughtful gift for anyone whut's my size, and they don't smell much."

But the Honky-Nark said, "What use would them shoes be to me? I got four feet, and you got two; you ain't got enough shoes for me."

But Little Black Charles said, "Lessee you got four feet! I don't see but two. You almost human."

"You gotta believe whut I tell you, son," the Honky-Nark said, "and don't give me none of your lip!"

Then the Honky-Nark put his hand on the handle of a flat, vicious-lookin', blued-steel, eleven-shot, .38-caliber Colt automatic pistol that lay in his holster.

Before the Honky-Nark could draw his pistol out, Little Black Charles had made a clean getaway, the package still secure under his arm. He ran away, sayin', "I still ahead of the game, I got my clothes, and I got the goods, and I'm on my way, but I don't rightly know if I want to be that all grand in the jungle: maybe it grander to be grand on the beach." But that didn't slow him down none.

And by and by Little Black Charles came to a park at 135th and Convent Avenue. He was pooped from all that runnin' so he climbed into a tree to rest.

Presently he heard a horrible noise that sounded like "Nigrrrr-rrr-r-r-rrrrr, gr-r-r-r-rrrrrrrrrrr!" and it got louder and louder. "Oh, dear!" said little Black Charles, "there are all the Honky-Narks comin' back to eat me up. Whut shall I do?" So he stayed in the tree which hid him from view, and peeked down to see what them Honky-Narks was cookin' up.

And there he saw all the Honky-Narks fightin', and disputin' which of them should stake out in the park to "hit" Little Black Charles when he show up. And at last they all got so angry that they began tearin' each other's badges off'n their uniforms. And they came, rollin' and tumblin' right to the foot of the very tree where Little Black Charles was hidin'. And as he became more and more amused at the goin's-on of the Honky-Narks, his grip on the package loosened, and down it fell, right among the wranglin', tanglin' Honky-Narks. And so Little Black Charles climbed down out of the tree and hid behind a rock. And the Honky-Narks didn't care a snit about Little Black Charles anymore. They was fightin' for that special delivery H what had fell out of the tree. But one didn't dare let the other loose, so they held on for dear life. And they were so angry, that they ran around the tree, tryin' to eat each other up with their big white teeth, and they ran faster and faster, till they were whirlin' around so fast that you couldn't see their legs at all.

And they stomped the contents of the package into the dust at their feet, till it disappeared. And still they ran faster and faster, till they all just melted away, and there was nothin' left but a great big pool of melted butter round the foot of the tree.

"Oh!" said Little Black Charles, "what lovely melted butter! I'll take that home to Black Mamma for her to cook with, and then she be the happiest black mamma in the jungle."

So he put it all into his pockets, and took it home to Black Mamma to cook with.

When Black Mamma saw the melted butter, she wasn't so pleased. "Now," said she, "where you git this rancid oil frum?"

And Little Black Charles told her the whole wonderful story, upon which she began to tremble with fear.

"Boy," she said, "you gonna hafta go away frum the jungle . . . far away! When that pusher find out that his dope is fertilizin' the shrubbery up at 135th and Convent, he gonna be after your ass, to put it politely."

So she got flour and eggs and milk and sugar, which she had been savin' for a grand occasion, and she made a big plate of most lovely pancakes. And she fried them in the melted margarine which tastes like the more expensive spread, and they were just as yellow and brown as the ones you get at B & G's.

And they both sat down to supper. Little Black Charles felt far from grand, he felt real bad. But his mamma's pancakes was so good and he was so hungry, that he ate a hundred and sixty-nine, before he left to stay with his grandma and grandpa down South.

June is on tour. J has been put away for his own safety. This is his second hospital. The first was a traditional lockup: visitors had to pass a desk, get checked off a list, then were let single file into a big room used for receiving guests. Inmates and visitors sat at trestle tables on long wooden benches, gorging themselves on food that had been hastily ripped from ordinary paper bags. Open garbage containers sat like honored guests at the head of each table. . . . It did not surprise me to see lifeguards in nurse's uniforms, who used pitchforks instead of paddles to belabor the troubled waters of insanity.

"Did you get my crayons?" I ask J. And he keeps smiling.

When I ask the nurse about the missing crayons, she says that they are probably misplaced. I am sure they are. All the patients steal. They are cunning, they are stealthy . . . but they are observed.

I visit J at the more modern hospital. My God, there are so many windows, and none of them can be opened. The air conditioning is on. When I step out of the elevator there are no locked doors that must be unlocked before I reach J. He is in the recreation room. It looks like a living room, except that most of the people are wearing pajamas and bathrobe. One man sitting at the end of the couch seems to be sinking. Another man, a boy with a bald head, is dancing to music heard by himself alone; he crashes into me.

J is still smiling. He is allowed to keep his gifts, here. His fingers fan out on the table; between each one he places a crayon. He hears another visitor say something . . . his face lights up . . . he stands . . . bows to me . . . extends his hand: he believes me to be Marie Curie. He presents me with the crayons that have been transformed into pitchblende, and from which I isolate a new element: radium salts. During the visit we share the toils and tribulations of research: tear the paper off crayons, break them into impure masses, determine atomic weights and properties of both polonium and radium . . . we share with Becquerel the 1903 Nobel Prize in Physics for radioactivity work. And we scribble our discoveries on the torn pieces of paper that wrapped our food. J screams! He discovers a hole eating through his hand . . . the radium has done its dirty work. Visiting hour is over. An orderly pulls J away from me. I try to wash his tainted hand with tears. It is my new discovery; tears can't wash taint off. I am Marie Sklodowska Curie, but my tears cannot reach him.

They have taken my bright young assistant to an empty room with a surveillance window. They have taken off his clothes. They give him a playful pat on the behind before they lock the door behind them. He crouches in a corner, holding the hand away from him. It disintegrates before his very eyes, falling away down the line of his arm like a lit fuse. He knows that once it reaches his body, he will die.

◉

M says to me, "If you had slept with J, you would be very guilty now."

"Why do you say that?" I ask.

"You would blame yourself for his illness."

"No, I wouldn't. If I had slept with him, and I didn't, but if I had, it would have kept him sane longer; maybe given him some of the happiest moments of his life."

"Maybe," M says. I wonder whether I contributed to J's breakdown.

J, darling, I had intended to speak to you about how it is my seventeen-year-old soul that loves you, but something interferes: the threat in my home: M. It is almost impossible to live with a madman who seems sane. (Would it be easier to live with a sane man who seemed mad?) He hates me and yet he will not give me up. I envy you in your cell, because you have lost your mind; I can't lose mine. You know, whenever M gives me orders: "Undress . . . don't move . . . express terror!" I try to faint or go somewhere else in my head, but can't. I wish that something would happen to me so that I could be taken away . . . rescued.

I call M's penis "The Threat." It is waiting for me when I wake up; at night it attempts to beat me over the head. It hangs in the air as M says, "I don't know why I should feel this way. I'm very hostile." He has his club in his hand, and I either make him feel better, or I will get it! I have just come out of a dream myself. I do not want to have sex with him. I ask, "Do you have to urinate?"

"I knew you'd say that," he says.

"Well, I do," I say, getting up and going into the

bathroom. He stays in bed. It is going to be an unpleasant day.

○

If you build a mountain of sand, do not expect it to stay in one place. I laugh at this "deep" saying that I made up. After I laugh, I reflect that it has something to do with the disappearing solidity of my marriage.

○

One fly is in the kitchen with me. It is after that rotting fruit M stole from the school lunchroom. He is a scavenger like the gull. He does not like fruit. He asked me to make jams and jellies out of it. I don't know how to do that. So . . . the fruit rots.

J, I have a present for you . . . a sea-gull card. It squawks when you press the middle of the card. I have one last visit with you before you go to a hospital in upstate New York. Perhaps you can imagine that you are by the seaside, when the gull cries.

I thank my legs for carrying me to you.

"Legs, thank you."

"He's in here," the nurse says.

"This is the snack room," you say, making a malted. "I have a shelf in the refrigerator all to myself. June brings me milk, and cheese, and salami. I can come in here any time of the day or night and make myself a snack."

Other inmates are wandering around the kitchen with food and drink in their hands. The sun is melting a plate of butter on the windowsill. A nurse comes in. "Anybody want me to slice anything?" she asks. She has a knife in her pocket. Nobody pays any attention to her. She goes out.

"She's after my balls," J confides, biting into the whole salami.

"I don't think so," I say in all sanity.

"YOU don't think so!" It enrages J. He whips open his bathrobe. "Look at this!"

It is not time to faint with delight. He has managed to stuff his entire complement of genitalia between his legs. He looks like a girl. I want to force his legs open, to show him he's still there.

"It isn't the first time," he says. "She takes them away."

"What does she do with them?" I ask.

"She gives them to the chief pathologist, who is in love with her. He turns them to glass . . . she looks into them and foretells the future, which is evil."

"Your balls have never been crystal clear to me," I say. "They're full of milky-white sperm."

"They used to be full of sperm!" he shouts. "But now she has released them to the female ward. . . . I'm fucking the whole world, but I'll never see my children."

"Where is your father?" I ask.

"He disappeared into Florida, he deserted me," J sobs.

"And whose fault is that?" I try to comfort him. I retrieve his penis, his balls . . . caress them in silence.

"It's the fault of the Tourist Bureau. They want everyone to travel," he reasons.

J has accused the Catholic Church of diverting man's vital energy to the service of a corpse. He escaped from the bus that was taking him to the asylum, and went directly to Riverside Church where a service was about to begin. He climbed the pulpit and shouted over the microphone: "Science is my universe!" A great organ started to play and drowned out his voice.

144

The doctor has given June a copy of his report on the neuropsychiatric examination of J.

Conclusions:

A) Egocentric, with a passionate tendency aimed at the reform of society, indignation of an erotic origin, vehemence, desire to draw attention to his "just" cause, love of theatrical attitudes, impulsive, need of instant satisfaction, pays no heed to the consequences of his act, paranoic logic. Autodidactism, militant philosophico-culture, with motorized white guilt, but no out-let, and no organized striking force. No belief in his existence. Personal annoyance on this point. Refutation of history. Denial of the future. Belief in a nonverbal present. Ambiva-lent, frenzied idealism. Accelerated contempt of religion, and those over thirty years of age. Lack of precogitation.

B) Markedly maniacal. Bursts of laughter. Excita-bility. Attacks, makes judgments, consigns to nothingness that which he declares does not exist. Naïve. Passes from one extremity to an-other. Proud and ashamed. At times wallowing in the splendor of his audacity. Does not per-ceive that his rebellion is thin stuff actually directed against a father figure. Resultant an-guish.

C) Schizoid. Appears intellectual, but merely gives lip service to scientific terms, and socioeconomic theories. This is a protective device which entangles him in conflict, and creates insoluble anxiety. He submits to uncertainty. Enters into depressive states. Takes refuge in a dissident society, which rejects him also. Onanism shamefacedly admitted.

Heterosexuality vehemently ascribed to, while entertaining homosexual fantasies.

May be pretending mental invalidism to prevent his induction into the army.

Present oculocardiac reflexes indifferent. Very strong tendinous and muscular reactions. Wants to strike out. Trembling in tongue and fingers when he does so. Hypermotivity. Intelligent. A didactic tone hostile to originality.

Possibility of a cure following a fit of modesty. Future not without promise, after a long term in asylum.

Jay Wolff remains a danger to public tranquillity. His condition requires that he be confined in an asylum, where he can receive the treatment of which he is in need.

Manhattan, 3/24/70

J and I are in disguise. We are on the lam. We make a modishly dressed couple. I am wearing hip-length boots, leather coat, a helmet, and a pants suit. He is wearing a pink pastel sack suit, purple wide-brimmed felt hat, and a frilled, cuff-linked, mauve striped shirt. He is perfumed, and relaxed in a pair of tapered shoes with stacked heels. We have shoulder-length hair. Our silhouettes are indistinguishable.

🌐

"How did you find us?" I ask Charles Thomas.

"I got ways," he says enigmatically.

"Why did you find us?" I open the windows to let out the fusty smell of love and careless "boo."

"I got reasons," he says. "Ask me to sit down. I'm here, ain't I?"

"Please sit down." I take Charles's coat and hang it on a chair.

"Got a present for you," he says, and thrusts a box at me.

"What's in it?" I ask.

"Find out," he says proudly. J passes him a joint. He sucks it in so deeply that the ash reaches his lips.

I unwrap a plastic turtle bowl.

A small rock.

A plastic palm tree.

Decorative plastic chips.

"Where's the turtle?" I ask.

147

"Right here." Charles Thomas has been holding the turtle in his pocket. He draws it out. It tries to crawl off his hand.

I put water in the bowl. Not too much. Just enough.

I put the turtle in the bowl and he sinks. Then he floats: a fragile unopened pillbox. His skinny little neck comes out cautiously. Then his feet. His right foot does not have claws. It looks as if some other turtle chewed them off. Each tiny bright eye observes what is on each side of it: our shadows, the rock, the rounded plastic sides of the bowl.

"What does it eat?" I ask Charles Thomas.

"Anythin'," he says, "chopped meat, tuna, lettuce, chicken, bugs . . . live bugs is best."

At the mention of live bugs, J laughs uproariously. This is a fine time to introduce J and Charles Thomas.

"Charles—J, J—Charles."

They take no notice of each other.

J begins to search for live bugs to feed the turtle. He is looking under cushions, under the rug, in the bed, in the stove . . . everywhere. And J laughs uproariously. Naturally; it's a lot of fun to go hunting in your own pad. J is sharp, but he has slowed down. He thinks he's fast. He doesn't catch anything, but it's still fun. He likes searching. I hadn't realized that before, how much J needs to look for something.

Maybe he's looking for lost love.

Maybe he's looking for love he never had.

Maybe he believed me when I described M as a cockroach and wants to squash him. But no, J is a naturalist, a scientist, an observer rather than an activist: he wants to find the food to feed the turtle.

Charles finds an old piece of salami in the fridge. He drops it into the turtle bowl. The turtle takes his first bite of the dim bit of meat, does not chew (does it have teeth?), but by progressive waves of contraction and relaxation of its neck (tubular, muscular), the food goes down.

Charles puts the bowl on the windowsill.

"Turtle needs sun," he says.

The turtle climbs the rock, closes its slow lidded eyes, draws its head forward toward the sun. The touch of the sun excites it: it stretches its limbs to rid itself of a lingering chill. Companionless, he sleeps.

"What is there to know about this turtle?" I ask Charles.

"Not much," he says, but he is not a student of turtles. Yet he has some opinions about it. "The turtle feels the hot or the cold. He feels fear and hunger. You can tell he were hungry by the way he eat. If he see us he try to hide. Look at this!"

Charles Thomas peers into the bowl. The turtle dives into the water; tries to squeeze himself between the side of the bowl and the rock. He stays sidewise and still.

"If he cold, he get in the sun," Charles Thomas continues. "If he cain't get in the sun, he go to sleep till it get warm. He ain't got no temperature of his own. So always test the water before you put him into it."

"You've been talking to the man in the pet store," I say.

"He's the expert," Charles Thomas says. "I want you to take good care of this here turtle; it's the first live thing I ever got you . . . outside of myself . . . and you ain't took too good a care of me, baby."

J has fallen asleep on the kitchen floor. Charles Thomas, my own dorsal carapace, hardens above me.

"Not yet," I say, "I'm not ready."

He takes one of my breasts in his mouth. He starts at the nipple and somehow the rest of the breast is sucked in. He covers me again. This is fair housing. He screams in Motown: "Baby, it's all right!" Both of us know it isn't. Masochistically I decide to bring us closer to the truth. I shout, "Nigger! Nigger! Nigger!" Every time I do, I get hotter and hotter. I expect punishment. Sure enough Charles Thomas removes himself from me with gentlemanly unhaste; stands at the side of the couch (on which I lie, my eyes begging forgiveness). He directs a powerful stream of piss at me. It is an elegant gesture, glimpsed through lace; an invitation to the dance.

Yellow foam splashes against my flesh: it reminds me of the dirty tide washed up on beaches too close to town.

"Sink or swim," Charles Thomas suggests paternally.

"I don't know what came over me," I say to him.

"I came over you," he explains.

Looking into the kitchen: "That white boy done caught enough turtle food for a month."

Creepy-crawly things are traversing the quiet form of J. His pockets are alive. His knuckles dance. His hair rises and falls. His nostrils, full of funky feelers, feed snot to the invaders.

"Is he dead?" I ask horrified.

"He the host; wouldn't be right for him to be dead," Charles Thomas says. "But it sure do look as if he lost control."

⬤

"I can't handle the lunchroom anymore," M says to me.

"Why not?" I refrain from telling M that he can't handle anything.

"The students keep demanding the microphone to broadcast their incendiary remarks, and when I give it to them, they shout that they haven't been given the microphone. Then . . . half the students troop out after some damn revolutionary, and the rest eat cold food and buy dope. That's the picture . . . that's the situation . . . I'm up to here with the whole thing!"

"Up to where?"

"Up to here!" He makes a slicing movement across

his throat from ear to ear. I hold a platter to receive his head. He is still alive, and insists on speaking. ". . . and the poetry they entertain each other with . . . society should have a right to protect itself from this type of filth, which is filth for the sake of filth and nothing else!"

Rebellion must be a heady wine! Multitudes come out of obscurity and are identified, and they send the enemy into oblivion in their turn. Is this what is happening at M's school? And what has dope got to do with it? I wouldn't mind turning on . . . building dream castles through whose empty halls I could hear my own laughter, and J's.

◉

The school lunchroom; the pusher has brought his violin. He has goods for sale of an amazing clarity and range. Five hundred students eager to make a connection have filled the lunchroom to capacity. Orchestral forces have been deployed across the room, for this occasion, in normal concert fashion. It is a cultural event.

A single microphone is suspended approximately eighteen feet above the platform from which M usually surveys the eaters . . . it is now a podium. The pusher stands slightly to the left of M. He is the soloist. He wears white tails and bow tie. Charles Thomas has made a painstaking effort to achieve perfect balance between solo and tutti. I am located at the precise aural focal point of the lunchroom.

The warning bell sounds. The pusher warms up. His violin tuned, he begins.

The violin concerto opens with a serene melody in B minor. Table B lights up and joints are passed around above pulsating chords on the harp, lower strings pizzicato and a sustained horn note. Three monitors pass out sticks of incense. There is still a slight smell of cabbage and coffee in the lunchroom. It is a noble spacious theme, to which intervals of the fourth lend a characteristically Acapulco flavor. I am turned on. I am in danger of giggling. I bite into a cube of sugar. It sparkles like a snowflake, and melts. M is conducting with a light-tipped baton, since the concert may last into evening.

The lyrical flow is interrupted by a restless motive, building up to table F (finance). Money and bodies are exchanged, restating the original theme in a fiscal relationship. Secondary ideas: paranoia about getting busted emphasize the thematic conflict as the movement develops in true classical sonata fashion. The pusher plays on, he knows what to expect. His chin grips the violin. His shoulder in a perpetual shrug supports it. His fingering is superb. He no longer needs a tourniquet to find the vein. No such technical legerdemain is required. In an intimate and subtle manner, the pusher spreads piquant coke on the shiny body of his violin and snorts it in. There is scattered applause by those not familiar with the piece . . . it is not over. Tablespoons are distributed to those requiring them, and souvenir packs of matches are tossed by the handful like wedding rice to the recently wedded. A promise of bliss is in the air, as the finale begins its savage introduction. Harmony is based on the pizzicato accompaniment to the opening theme of the first movement, when things were light and gay. In a more primitive mood, the pusher removes his clothing and dances. He is sodomized as M's baton probes for deeper meaning.

Charles Thomas envelops me between two allegro movements. We are tranquil in this haunting, songlike movement: post-mainline, present high. Having scored a sparse, delicate, and transparent taste of death, we die. Five hundred students, each a short variation on a theme, unable to stand the pure stuff, die with us.

The pusher and M see that their audience has gone. They turn down the amps. Amazingly they sing a poignant lament. It is superfluous.

⬤

"Still making it with the kid?" Lita asks. I don't care to tell her that the "kid" is all memories and much daydreaming.

J takes my lipstick and writes on the bathroom mirror the words: FUCK JAY.

He is out on a weekend pass. I would like to go to The Cloisters with him but the Unicorn Tapestry makes J froth at the mouth, "The horn is too sharp and spirally," he says.

"It's a mythical beast, it can't hurt anyone," I say.

"There's a rip in the tapestry that's been mended," J points out. "The unicorn is not tame!" He seems terrified of the beautiful white horse with the lion's tail, sporting in a hunting park with ladies.

"The unicorn can be tamed by a virgin. It's symbolic of chastity and purity," I say to soothe J.

"There are no virgins, and it will never be tamed," he insists.

"Why did you write FUCK JAY on my mirror?" I ask.

"I really wanted to write FUCK MELISSA, but I used my name instead so you wouldn't be mad at me."

"Why do you feel that way about me? Aren't we friends? You told me that no matter what happened we would always be friends." It is unfair of me to pretend I am merely a friend. I may not be a friend at all. I may be his enemy. It depends on what action I take.

"We are friends," J says, "but I'm not your lover boy anymore."

"I know that J. I accept your decision."

He is examining his hands which have broken out into a rash. They itch him. I offer to bring him calamine lotion.

"I don't mind if they itch," J says. "I like it. I scratch and it feels great. The doctor isn't worried about my skin. He says it's just a minor symptom."

J scratches till he bleeds. I find myself kissing J's hands. They are pressed to my mouth and I am licking his blood. It has a familiar taste.

"June doesn't love me," J says suddenly, glaring at me.

"Yes she does love you, J. She talks about you all the time, and she's planning to buy you an enlarger."

"She has a boyfriend," J sobs. "She took him to her new studio at night and they made love."

"So what!" I say stupidly.

"What does she need him for!" he shouts in anguish.

"What do you mean, J, darling . . . oh, darling, what do you mean?"

He pulls away from me and buries his head in the drapes. "What does she need him for when she's got me?"

Two stark walls. An uninhabited, unfinished room. A tremulous half-light coming through large loft windows. The floor has been newly laid. It is pine. The pine has been waxed many times to bring out the natural beauty of the wood. Such a floor rejects liquids that spill on it. It is the floor of a dancer.

A woman wearing a silver helmet, out of which protrudes a long mane of black hair, enters from an open side of the room. She is naked. On her breasts are pinned two buttons. The motto: MAKE WAR, NOT LOVE.

A man enters from the opposite side of the unfinished room. He walks with the measured tread of a dancer pretending he is walking.

The woman is swaying gently. When she stops moving, her flesh continues, as if in slow motion. She lies down on the floor, her body stretched full length, running from one wall to the other. She is an animal trap. She waits for an undomesticate. She listens for a roar, or, a creaking of the floor, or, the stealthy opening of a door.

The man trips over her body. He falls upon it. He bites the nape of her neck.

She cries out in passion, "Ohhhhhhhhhhhh!" The sound is guttural, it goes on and on; she hardly seems to hear it. Then it is snipped from her mouth and "Ohhhh-hhhhhh!" floats like a banner across the room.

She turns her head. It is June. Her helmet, still intact

upon her head, has sprouted two ivory horns. The horns light up (low-wattage nite-lights lead the lover to her). He grasps the horns for balance as he throws himself upon her. He overflows within her. Juice, sweat, and semen stream to the corners of the room and pool there. Aroused, June drinks up the corners. Shadows disappear.

The man follows her in the manner of a dancer pretending to walk. He crouches over her in the manner of a man pretending to fuck. He turns his head.

It is M!

He has choreographed his way into her body.

They go to the exercise bar. As their knees bend, their arms drift out gracefully.

What a weird couple they make.

◉

The block is sealed off. Crouching fuzz are everywhere. An officer with a bullhorn to his lips is shouting orders. There is movement behind cars, and guns aiming at our windows. Violent shafts of light turn in a fiery arc, illuminating the sky and the building where we're hiding. Every time the light makes one of its wide, crazy sweeps, I flatten under the table . . . M hugs the wall.

It has been several hours since the police laid siege.

Lew Harris is down there talking to the chief of police.

Hundreds of people have gathered behind police barricades.

A squad of police are trying to keep them in order.

A lady runs from the front rank of the crowd toward our building. She is tackled by a burly officer. He appears to dry-hump her as she turtles away. Another policeman is playing xylophone by striking, with his small wooden nightstick, the shinbones of those who dare to surge forward.

J lies dead on the stairs.

Two policemen are outside the door, one on each side . . . waiting.

M catches sight of himself in the mirror, and shoots. The mirror cracks. My sculpture of Sirius is showered with glass.

"Why don't you give yourself up!" I shout at M.

The cop with the bullhorn is admonishing the crowd in a rapid, one-note voice: "Go home. Everybody go home! It is dangerous to remain in the area. This is an order. Leave immediately!"

For the first time the crowd is still: nobody moves an inch. Another squad of police come charging up and try to push them back. The crowd allows itself to be hustled and shoved . . . but only into another shape: rhomboid into parallelogram into equilateral triangle.

I am not frightened. I know that I will be rescued.

J meets a lady outside his school. She asks him, "Would you like to learn an instrument?"

"Yes," he answers.

"What instrument would you like to play?" She stands, pencil poised above a yellow lined pad.

"Guitar," he says. For a moment, the hope that he can be like the others, a boy of his time, exalts his dreary outlook.

She inscribes the information. "And what is your name?"

"Jay Wolff."

He gives her his address and telephone number. She thanks him and approaches other children leaving the school: "Would you like to learn an instrument . . . ?"

A few weeks later, June answers the doorbell; it is the woman from the music school. "Yes?" June asks. "What do you want?"

"I understand that your son wants to learn to play the guitar . . ."

"My son is no longer with me," June says.

The woman, embarrassed, withholds the rest of her sales pitch. "You mean he is not coming back?" she inquires, already ringing for the elevator.

"He's not coming back, ever!" June says.

Now, June experiences the shock of J's death as if he

had died in the war and sent her a cheerful letter which she receives posthumously.

Should June believe the letter or the corpse?

🌀

"Do you believe in ghosts?" I ask J.

"Yes," J answers, "so does Mummy and Letitia."

"Are you afraid of them?"

"No . . . I like them. Ghosts are disembodied spirits wandering among us because they want to make their presence known: they are spiritual beings who died young and still have things to say."

"Have you ever communicated with a specter?"

"No, but when I die I'll communicate with you," J promises.

"Please communicate with me now," I beg.

I am not sure I will be able to receive his messages. I am not in the least receptive to the idea that he will die. And, I have never been visited by a ghost before. My television, however, has often played host to a pale, double image, appearing on the screen as a white shadow.

. . . Melt . . .

Embalmer: We use the lost-wax method. No fine line lost. This smile set in wax lasts forever.

Me: But isn't waxed the opposite of waned? And, where is the emotion that animates the line? Why has death sealed his lips when he promised to come back to me from the dead!

. . . Melt . . .

M and I are conducting the remaining business of marriage in a colony of sun and surf worshipers; we are strange invaders to this sleepy strand of beach. When I can't stand M, I jump into the ocean and let the waves thunder over me, or I lie on the beach and watch the young men flex their muscles and/or ride their surfboards into shore. This is the easy life, bringing a dilettante corpse to life every day (M). He tries: imitating the great breakers, he crashes monotonously into me through the hot days and cooler nights, but he is a wave in a bathtub.

162

We live in a white stucco house with a red tile roof. We are scarcely visible behind date and cypress trees . . . a wall surrounds a courtyard and fountain. From our living-room window can be seen the sapphire-blue Atlantic, into which M tosses salted peanuts.

We dine alfresco on an outdoor terrace, under a pink and yellow beach umbrella. M is certain that the dark-green lobster I bought for our dinner tonight is a sign.

"What kind of a sign?" I ask him.

"A warning to me . . . that all lobsters are alive before they are dead," he replies.

I notice for the first time, M encased in a suit of armor made of hard shell. The front part of his body is practically solid; the rest of the shell is divided into seven segments, the last of which forms the coccyx.

"Why would I bring you such a sign?" I am ready to deny it, but I have often been the intermediary between supernatural powers and mortals.

"You were merely the agent . . . Jay used you to get at me!"

"Then you don't blame me?"

M waves his great claws within inches of my nose. One of the claws is thick and heavy: for crushing tender objects. The other is more slender, curved, and provided with many sharp teeth. M does not seize me with it. He seems resigned.

J has come for me, riding the broad back of a giant sea turtle. They have remained afloat for fifteen hours, skimming the surface of the water. I am waiting on the shore with a blanket, and a Thermos of hot beef bouillon. The wind is tossing bits of orange paper around on the beach; it is the lobster J made for me. As he approaches, I wonder whether the monster he is hanging on to isn't the same turtle Charles Thomas once gave me, but which M threw into the toilet bowl? If alligators are discovered full grown in sewers, why can't the same be true of discarded turtles?

Although J has come for me, he is merely an escort, acting as emissary for the nether world. Protocol must be observed.

"Do you have a note to leave M?" J asks stiffly.

"It's in this yellow purse." I show it to J.

"Leave it on the beach. Here, put this rock on it." He gives me a rosette of tabular crystals of barite, enclosing sand grains and colored by iron oxide.

"It's too beautiful to leave behind," I say.

" 'Barite roses' are common enough," J answers, "I'll get you another. Are you going to leave your clothes on?"

"What do you suggest?"

"Leave them on. They'll act as a weight when you're

ready to sink. If you begin to change your mind, it'll be too late to struggle out of them."

The turtle sips beef bouillon before we mount her. She flips sand over my purse which makes a mound on the beach resembling an egg. When the sun comes to warm the beach tomorrow, M will stumble on my purse, and find its contents pregnant.

"Let's go!" J shouts.

The wind has risen and is blowing waves horizontally so that I have to keep my head down. I am riding in front of J. His arms are around me. I shield my eyes from the sharp spray by pressing my hand against my forehead. I can see only a few inches ahead of me. Though the turtle knows the way, she hesitates for a moment, then looks back at J for instructions. He prods the soft spot under her tail. She changes direction; vertical, disappears under the waves with us. I observe dim circles of light behind my eyelids, as if I had been struck. Falling fast, the light grows dimmer and dimmer . . . my skirt billows around my thighs . . . bubbles and ears, pop . . . J floats away, a silver button in his fist. The turtle dives again. There is complete silence.

M lights a shaking cigarette as he reads the note I
have left for him. He smooths the paper on his knee:

Is suicide my only alternative? Is being nothing
in life, comparable to being nothing in death?

decided to kill myself
at the age of thirty-nine since I
have experienced nothing
of life that was yearned for.

& I wouldn't think
of leaving you M

for someone, that is.

while Lita and June went
into activities, preparing
their bodies for actions of love
I skimmed the surface

& was bored.
                              Conclusion?

spent fifteen years as an
apprentice wife
preparing for   ?
in "the real world"

                    From,
                    "It is Melissa I mourn for."

P.S. We are HERE now in the shark's fin soup
         after having fooled ourselves about the

steaming present. Our thanx (J too) to
you for having allowed this accomplishment.

> Good-bye Mark
> I'm going back inside my head,
> or did you think that I was
> really dead?

ABOUT THE AUTHOR

Novelist, playwright, painter, Rosalyn Drexler lives in New York City with her husband and two children. She is the author of a novel, *I Am the Beautiful Stranger* and of a collection of plays entitled, *The Line of Least Existence.*